Searching for Mr. Cyber-Right

Soozie hated to admit it even to herself, but it was definitely fun navigating her way into the chat room. Now to pick the absolutely perfect screen name. For a moment, she felt as blank as the screen, then she began to grin. "SSS," she finally typed, loving her new name, Stylish Sister Soozie.

"What's it stand for?" Nick asked.

"You still there?" Soozie whirled around. "This is supposed to be private."

"Thanks to you, too," he said, shaking his head. She watched until he disappeared behind the next bank of terminals, then leaned toward her screen. After a long moment, inspiration struck. "Here goes nothing," she muttered.

Anyone out there in cyberland? Anyone single and male, that is, who thinks chatting up a stranger on a Saturday night—sight unseen—can be fun? Oh, and only *mature* Wilder men need apply. Seniors okay. Grad students better. SSS

NANCY DREW ON CAMPUS™

Available from ARCHWAY Paperbacks

Nancy Drew
on campus™ #19

Love On-Line

Carolyn Keene

AN ARCHWAY PAPERBACK
Published by POCKET BOOKS
New York London Toronto Sydney Tokyo Singapore

AN ARCHWAY PAPERBACK *Original*

An Archway Paperback published by
POCKET BOOKS, a division of Simon & Schuster Inc.
1230 Avenue of the Americas, New York, NY 10020

Copyright © 1997 by Simon & Schuster Inc.
Produced by Mega-Books, Inc.

ISBN: 0-671-00211-2

First Archway Paperback printing March 1997

10 9 8 7 6 5 4 3 2 1

NANCY DREW, AN ARCHWAY PAPERBACK and colophon are registered trademarks of Simon & Schuster Inc.

NANCY DREW ON CAMPUS is a trademark of Simon & Schuster Inc.

Cover photos by Pat Hill Studio

Printed in the U.S.A.

IL 8+

CHAPTER 1

"Has the guilt set in yet?" Terry Schneider asked Nancy Drew as they ducked out the side door of Wilder University's Hewlitt Performing Arts Center and into the windy night.

Nancy drew in a deep breath of winter air and looked up at the sky, bright with stars. The cold energized her, and she felt light and happy—so happy that she almost didn't miss being with her boyfriend, Jake Collins. Almost.

"Why should I feel guilty?" Nancy replied cheerfully, stopping to button her navy blue pea coat and trying to put aside all thoughts of Jake. After all, she *had* asked him to join her tonight for the opening of the Focus Film Society's Italian movie festival, and Jake had turned *her* down.

"You just kidnapped the president of the FFS," Terry teased. He wore a thick woolen sweater with holes in the elbows, and no coat, but he seemed perfectly warm. His cheeks were a healthy pink and his eyes sparkled.

"Rescued, not *kidnapped,"* Nancy said, tossing her red-blond hair off her face. "I just saved you from a fate worse than death—inside that over-heated screening room, leading a postfilm discussion group."

"I love watching movies and talking about them, but sometimes the film freaks get way too serious. You should have heard the discussion after the cartoon festival this fall."

"How much could they find to pick apart about Bugs Bunny?" Nancy asked, matching her stride to his as they headed for Java Joe's.

"They totally killed 'dat wabbit.' " He clutched at his heart and staggered toward the coffeehouse.

"You're nuts," Nancy said. She smiled and shook her head as Terry held the door to the coffee shop open.

"I did want to talk about tonight's movie," she added, stepping in from the cold and letting the warm fragrance of espresso envelop her.

"Me, too." Terry looked around the crowded hangout. "But talking privately over cappuccino and Italian pastries sounds more interesting than an intellectual group discussion."

Nancy raised her eyebrows. "Private? Here?"

Terry smiled. "Skip private. Let's settle for one-on-one."

While Terry went to the counter to order two cappuccinos and biscotti, Nancy grabbed a table by the window and took off her coat. After smoothing her black miniskirt over her tights, she crossed her long legs.

"Did anyone ever tell you you always look great?" Terry said, setting their drinks down.

Nancy blushed at his compliment and lowered her gaze. She'd known Terry for a couple of months now; even though she considered him just a friend, she had to admit she was attracted to him. Except for his light sandy hair, Terry was a dead ringer for Nancy's ex-boyfriend, Ned Nickerson. Nancy was beginning to wonder if Terry's allure had something—or everything—to do with the similarities.

"You seem a little down." Terry reached out and touched Nancy's arm. "The sad ending got to you?"

"Sad ending?" Nancy snapped out of her thoughts. "Oh, of the movie, you mean. No, no. Not that." She moved her arm away and warmed her fingers around her cup. "Besides, I'm not sad."

"Come on, Nancy. I can see you're unhappy. If it's not the movie, then it must be Jake."

Nancy looked up quickly. Terry met her gaze and held it. Terry had made it clear just after they'd met that he was definitely interested in her. But Nancy had told him Jake and she were serious. At the time it seemed impossible that she'd ever have problems with Jake. "It *is* Saturday night. . . ." Terry added, a hopeful note in his voice.

"Nothing's wrong between me and Jake, Terry. He's just not into foreign films."

Nancy decided she wasn't going to waste one more second of the evening worrying about Jake. It was his fault he was missing out on the fun tonight, not hers.

She lifted her mug of cappuccino toward Terry. "Let's toast the first night of your film festival."

"I'll drink to that," Terry said.

They clinked their cups together. Feeling more relaxed, Nancy sat back, sipped her coffee, and began to talk movies with someone who shared her enthusiasm.

"I thought by the time I was a senior I'd have the whole guy thing figured out." Janie Covington confided to Bess Marvin. The two girls were sprawled on the thick rug in front of the living room fireplace of the Kappa sorority house.

Unlike everyone else in the house, neither of them had plans for the evening, and Bess was thoroughly enjoying sorting out Janie's guy troubles. Talking about someone else's dating problems took Bess's mind off her own broken heart. Her boyfriend, Paul Cody, had died recently in a tragic accident, and whenever she thought about him, the hurt inside was almost unbearable.

Bess forced her mind off Paul and back to her sorority sister's problems. "I think you should just ask him out," she declared.

"How? I barely know him. He's in one of my

classes, but I never see him anywhere else. And I have a feeling he doesn't even know I exist."

Bess thought a moment, studying Janie. She didn't know the Kappa senior well, but she liked her. Janie was a little quiet and definitely a little offbeat. A performance artist, she really dressed the part, with a thrift-shop wardrobe that was mismatched and funky. Bess was impressed that Janie could pull it off with such flair.

Janie's curly dark hair framed her big green eyes and delicate features. Bess envied her lean body, even though some of the Kappa sisters thought Janie was a little too thin. She wondered why the guys in Janie's classes didn't fall all over her.

"Take a chance," Bess declared. "Next time you see him, walk up to him and ask him out."

"You're right," Janie said. Then abruptly she wailed and buried her face in her hands. "I can't! I don't have the nerve."

"Sure you do," Bess said. "Invite him to brunch at the Bumblebee Diner or coffee at Java Joe's."

Janie groaned. "You make it sound so easy."

"It's easier than worrying about how to get to know him," Bess said.

"That might be true for you, Bess," Janie said, getting up and putting another log on the fire, "but not for me. I can't even speak to a guy I don't know without blushing." Janie gave an embarrassed laugh and rearranged the fire screen.

Bess wasn't sure what to say. She had seen Janie, with an installation artist, perform at Hewlitt a couple of months ago, and Janie had been outrageously funny, loud, and uninhibited. But in small groups, even among her sorority sisters, she was shy, sometimes even defensive.

Bess watched the flames dance in the fireplace and basked in the warmth of the fire. She loved the Kappa house and the warm feeling she got from hanging out with her sorority sisters. Bess kicked off her shoes and propped her feet up on the sofa. "If I were an upperclassman, I'd live here," she said. "How come you don't?"

Janie hesitated. "By the time you're a senior, group living wears kind of thin," she said stiffly. "There's no privacy in a sorority house."

Personally, Bess adored the commotion and liveliness of the old Victorian mansion. She couldn't wait until sophomore year, when she'd have a chance to move in.

"Anyone want to sample some brownies?" a voice asked from the kitchen door.

Bess looked up and saw a plump, pretty girl, a Kappa sister she didn't know very well.

Janie's face lit up. "Leila, don't tell me you're still trying to fatten up the Kappas!" Janie turned to Bess. "Have you guys met? Leila's a voice major."

"Would-be opera singer!" Leila smiled warmly at Bess and offered her a brownie. "And I'm not trying to fatten *anyone* up. I baked two batches of these to bring to the guys in Mitch's band."

She turned to Bess. "He's a jazz pianist I've worked with—"

"Who happens to be gorgeous *and* her boyfriend," Darcy Flanagan informed Bess as she walked up to snag a brownie from the tray. The leggy dance major joined Bess and Janie around the fire.

"He's playing at Club Z tonight, and I promised I'd bring these for a party afterward." Leila set down the tray and settled on the couch behind Bess.

"Actually, it's payback. He got passes to the club and some of us are tagging along with Leila. Want to come?" Darcy said in invitation to Bess and Janie.

"Can't," Janie said. "I'm heading straight home from here to work out the kinks in the computer program for the visuals in my next piece."

"And it's time for me to hit the books back at the dorm," Bess said, not in the mood for a night at Club Z.

"I knew I smelled brownies!" Soozie Beckerman cried, coming down the stairs. She tossed her beige cashmere sweater onto a chair next to Darcy, sat down, and helped herself to a brownie.

"Your cast is off," Soozie said to Bess, a flicker of sympathy lighting her ice blue eyes. "How's your arm?"

"Not bad," Bess said, rubbing her arm. She had broken it in the same accident that had killed Paul.

Soozie shifted her gaze from Bess to Janie. "Can't stay away, can you?" she said in a cool, amused voice.

"All Kappas are free to use the house, whether they live here or not," Janie replied tersely. "Or have you forgotten?"

"You seem to be the one with the bad memory. Have you forgotten that you're not welcome here?"

Bess groaned softly. She didn't know the source of the bad blood between them, but Janie and Soozie were always arguing about something. She jumped up, happy to see Holly Thornton coming in the front door.

"Who's that?" Leila murmured.

Behind Holly was a guy with black hair and amazing sky blue eyes. Bess hadn't been introduced to him, but she had seen him once, the day Holly first met him at Java Joe's.

"Hey, guys!" Holly said. She wore black heels and a short black dress. Her golden hair hung almost to her waist and her brown eyes glowed. She touched the guy's shoulder lightly and said, "I want you to meet Jean-Marc Chenier."

"Not the guy you met on-line!" Soozie blurted. The usually cool, controlled Soozie looked so surprised, Bess had to bite back a laugh.

Holly smiled sweetly at Soozie. "One and the same. This is the guy who 'wasn't worth meeting'—that is how you put it, isn't it?" Holly said, lacing her fingers through Jean-Marc's.

"Not exactly," Soozie said, coloring slightly. "I

8

just said I didn't think on-line dating was such a great idea."

"Oh. Why not?" Jean-Marc asked.

Soozie seemed at a loss for words but after a moment mustered up a thin smile. "Because you never know *whom* you might meet."

"And you're the authority," Janie said in a mocking tone.

Soozie glanced at her scornfully. "Any creep could be surfing the Net, you know."

Jean-Marc nodded. "True. So you have to be careful when you first meet in person. But in our case, it was worth the risk," he said. He turned back to Soozie and said earnestly, "You should try it sometime. It is a good way to make friends."

Bess winced and stole a glance at Soozie. Soozie's lips were pursed. Bess could tell Jean-Marc's comment was perfectly innocent, but Soozie looked insulted. Before she could respond, Jean-Marc whispered something in Holly's ear. Then he said to the other girls with a smile, "It was good meeting you, but we've got reservations for dinner."

"At Les Peches," Holly added, a tiny note of triumph in her voice. Jean-Marc zipped up his brown bomber jacket and followed Holly into the hall. As soon as the front door banged shut, Darcy pretended to fall back in a faint on the sofa. "Whoa, is he gorgeous!"

Leila nodded her agreement. "If I didn't have Mitch, I'd be tempted to try the Net myself."

"I still can't believe they met on-line," Soozie said, sounding a little sour. "And what did he mean by a good place to make friends? Does he think *I* have a problem meeting people?"

"I'm sure he didn't mean anything," Darcy said, hurrying to assure her.

Soozie laughed. "Launching a manhunt on the Net is not about to become my favorite pastime. But, Janie, maybe you should try it. You're the one too scared to ask your 'mystery guy' out."

"How do you know about him?" Janie blurted out, sending a panicky glance toward Bess.

"If something's private, don't talk about it in the sorority common room," Soozie shot back.

"It's true," Darcy said. "The walls have ears." She checked her watch. "Hey, it's getting late, and I want to get to Club Z to see what's happening in the guy department. I'm with Sooz on this one—I'd rather do my flirting in person," Darcy said, getting up.

"But you've got to admit, Holly did pretty well," Leila added.

Soozie shrugged. "Holly could use a little excitement in her life. She's been dateless for months now."

"And your datebook is jammed, I'm sure," Janie said sarcastically.

Soozie rose, picking up her sweater. "I'm sorry I can't stay for more of this fascinating conversation," she declared, and marched out of the room, her chin high. Bess watched her flounce upstairs. A moment later the door to her room slammed shut.

The girls exchanged glances.

"Was it something I said?" Janie asked innocently.

Everyone cracked up.

Darcy laughed, too, but shook her head. "You guys are too hard on her. Soozie's competitive and a bit of a snob, but she's a good person, really."

"You're entitled to your opinion," Leila said. "You two have been friends for ages."

"And Soozie needs all the friends she can get," Janie added.

Bess giggled with everyone else, but she wondered why Janie was so bitter.

Ray Johansson leaned into the microphone, and his dark eyes locked with Karin Messer's blue ones. His gravelly voice blended in perfect harmony with Karin's haunting mellow alto as they sang.

"Flame of love, fire or ice
  Love like ours won't happen twice
  I'll follow the rider of my dark dreams
  Love, like the moon, is not what it seems."

Karin tried to hold Ray's gaze as they let the last notes die out. Ray pointedly looked away, and as he strummed the final chord sequence, he signaled the end of the song with a nod toward Cory McDermott.

"Great!" Cory declared from behind his drum set. "That tune's really shaping up."

Karin shook her long bangs out of her eyes and winked at Ray. He shifted uncomfortably and tried to figure out when Karin had developed a crush on him. "It did go well," she agreed. "Our voices are a perfect fit, Ray."

"Time for a break? I'm starved," Cory said, casting a quick glance at Austin Rusche.

"Whatever!" Austin answered, vaguely annoyed. Ray watched, troubled, as Austin put down his guitar and ambled to the far side of the loft. Cory pulled sodas from the cooler and joined Austin. That left Ray paired up with Karin once again.

Bad move, Ray thought, straddling a chair. He smiled weakly as Karin handed him a cold drink. "Thanks." He studied Radical Moves' new vocalist as she hunted down a snack in her backpack. Karin was a terrific singer, an excellent musician, and a really great person. Her voice, like his, was dark and haunting; they did seem born to sing together. But Ray was beginning to think she spelled disaster for his new band.

Before Ray had joined Radical Moves, Karin had been dating Austin. Their breakup had wrecked the band, and the decision to let her rejoin after Ray came on board had not been easy. She and Austin had agreed to be civil, but

Karin's version of being civil was to pretend Austin didn't exist while she flirted with Ray.

Maybe it was his own fault. In his efforts to keep Karin and Austin apart, he had befriended the singer. But she'd been acting more than friendly.

"What do you say we check out that late-night jazz club over in East Weston after rehearsal tonight?"

Karin's suggestion jolted Ray. For a second the idea appealed to him. He was too wound up to go back to his dorm, but going out with Karin would give her the wrong idea. "Can't," he said.

"Studying on a Saturday night? You don't seem the type." Her strong voice echoed across the loft.

Ray wished she'd keep her voice down.

"Careful, or I might get the idea you don't want to spend time with me," Karin said, pouting prettily.

"Karin, I'm busy. That's all." Ray ignored his instinct to reassure her. He was determined not to jeopardize his relationship with this band. Besides, there was Ginny. In the depths of his heart, Ray was sure that some way, someday Ginny Yuen would be back with him. Karin might be the woman he sang his love songs *with,* but Ginny was the one he'd always sing them *to.*

Soozie sat in her room and stared bleakly at the last words she'd written in her diary: "When I'm Kappa president, I'm going to see to it that no one ever pledges this house who's a would-be opera singer—especially those who spend half their time baking. Leila Como has the wrong image for Kappa."

"Who are you kidding?" Soozie said to herself. Leila might be overweight, but she was talented and beautiful *and* she went with one of the cutest and coolest guys in Zeta. And Soozie, like it or not, was dateless for the third week in a row. As dateless as pathetic Janie Covington.

Thinking of Janie, Soozie quickly suppressed a pang of guilt. Last year she'd played a trick on Janie before Kappa's Spring Fling. Soozie thought it was pretty funny, but apparently Janie didn't have much of a sense of humor. Instead of laughing it off, Janie had ultimately moved out of the house. Soozie bit her lip, then shrugged. Some girls were just too thin skinned.

Soozie got up and walked over to her dresser. The face that met her eyes in the mirror was the stuff prom queens were made of: chiseled, angular cheekbones, wide-set blue eyes, a flawless creamy complexion, pale blond silky hair. Even after a good cry, her eyes were barely red, and her makeup was still perfect. But Leila and Holly had dates tonight; Soozie didn't.

She wasn't sure why, either. She had dated heavily her first two years at Wilder, and she'd gone out now and then this fall, but the guys seemed too young or unsophisticated. For the past three weeks, no one had even asked her out. Weird.

The memory of Janie's jibes about her empty datebook made her stomach knot up and thinking about her archrival, Holly Thornton, meeting a gorgeous guy on-line made it even worse. A moment later her hurt inspired her. She capped her fountain pen, closed the hand-bound journal and placed it under her checkbook, then she shut the desk drawer.

She touched up her lipstick and grabbed her coat. "I'll show them!" she said, sweeping down the side stairs and out the back door. How dare Janie lump her with the chronically dateless!

CHAPTER 2

As I suspected, computer geeks have nothing better to do than peer at their screens on Saturday nights, Soozie thought as she stood in the computer lab in the basement of Graves Hall. Most of the terminals were already taken.

"Can I help you?"

Soozie turned and looked up at a tall, lean guy in a denim shirt and jeans. His straight brown hair was longish in front. He tossed it out of his dark eyes, and smiled at her. For a second her heart began to pound, then she noticed his pocket protector, with three ballpoint pens neatly tucked into it, and her pulse dropped right back to normal.

She arched one carefully shaped eyebrow and read the laminated name tag pinned to his shirt: Nick O'Donnell, Systems Administrator. "Does that put you in charge?" she asked in her sweetest voice.

"Yeah, I'm on tonight. Looking for a computer?"

"That's why I'm here." Soozie forced a smile.

Nick pointed her to one just freeing up a few feet away.

"No." Soozie put on a pretty pout. "Something a little more *intime.*"

"Something what?" Nick knit his brow.

Soozie restrained a sigh and batted her lashes. "Intimate. Private."

"Oh." His smile broadened, and Soozie noticed his dimples. He motioned for her to follow. "So you know how to log on and all?" he asked, standing beside her as she took off her coat.

Soozie could sense him looking her over. He might be a computer geek, but still, she never minded a cute guy appreciating her. "Log on? Of course." She sat down and pushed up the sleeves of her sweater. "I'm no dummy, but—" Soozie started sharply, then softened her tone. "But I don't know a thing about getting on-line." She turned to face him, sure he'd mock her.

Instead he nodded sympathetically. "Where exactly do you want to go? Other university libraries? Magazine articles? Research topics?"

Embarrassed, Soozie hemmed and hawed. "No, not exactly. I . . . ummm . . . I need to talk to people. . . ." she finished lamely.

"Right," Nick said, completely unfazed. "You want to access the Usenet chat room. What subjects are you interested in?"

Soozie swallowed her pride. "Oh, who am I

kidding?" She looked at her hands. "I want to go where people make connections on campus."

"You do?" Nick sounded amazed. "You don't look like the type who needs to surf the Net to meet people."

Soozie felt a blush rise to her cheeks. "Who says I do? Maybe you should mind your own business. Now, are you going to help me, or do I have to register some sort of complaint?"

Nick threw up his hands. "Take it easy. I'll help you. Here's how you get to Usenet. It's the Wilder network where people exchange all sorts of messages and ideas. From there you can meet someone—uh—people with similar interests and go off to private rooms to chat." He told her to log on to the computer using the password she'd chosen back at registration in September. "Never use your password as your on-line screen name," he warned her. He told her to pick out a screen name and then helped her through the first steps of the process.

Soozie hated to admit it even to herself, but it was definitely fun navigating her way into the chat room. Now to pick the absolutely perfect screen name. For a moment, she felt as blank as the screen, then she began to grin. "SSS," she finally typed, loving her new name, Stylish Sister Soozie.

"What's it stand for?" Nick asked.

"You still there?" Soozie whirled around. "This is supposed to be private."

"Thanks to you, too," he said, shaking his

head. She watched until he disappeared behind the next bank of terminals, then leaned toward her screen. After a long moment, inspiration struck. "Here goes nothing," she muttered.

> Anyone out there in cyberland? Anyone single and male, that is, who thinks chatting up a stranger on a Saturday night—sight unseen—can be fun? Oh, and only *mature* Wilder men need apply. Seniors okay. Grad students better. SSS

Soozie sat back and watched her screen. For the longest time, nothing happened. Suddenly she was worried no one would talk to her. She was afraid that without being able to see her, no one would want to get to know her. How could she ever turn heads in the invisible world of Wilder's Usenet?

I am not going to cry. She pushed back her chair. *I'm outta here,* she thought, just as a string of characters flickered across the screen.

Soozie's heart leaped up as she leaned forward to read the message.

> SSS—I hear you. Loud and clear. Mysteries and heart-to-hearts on-line are definitely cool. TDH

TDH! Soozie chuckled quietly as she typed.

> TDH—Tall, Dark, Handsome—am I right? SSS

SSS—Not for me to say. See for yourself
someday in person. Meanwhile . . . what's your
thing? TDH

Soozie thought a moment. Suddenly she felt a
whole world open in front of her—sight unseen.
Name unknown, she could be anyone, anything
she had ever dreamed of. She typed the next
three words that popped into her head.

TDH—Looking for love!

Jake Collins turned up the collar of his leather
jacket and surveyed the Wilder campus from the
top steps of the Rockhausen Library. Everywhere
he looked he saw couples, arm and arm, criss-
crossing the campus walk. The world was in couple mode and Jake felt left out.

Since he and Nancy had started dating, they
had barely spent a Saturday night apart—until
recently.

A burger at a fast-food joint—*alone*—had not
been his plan tonight. He'd had a tough week,
and he had been longing for an intimate dinner
with Nancy at Eritrea, the candlelit Ethiopian
restaurant in town that they both loved. Nancy
had nixed the whole idea without a second
thought. She'd gotten it in her head to go to some
moody Italian film.

Jake was definitely not into Fellini; Nancy was.
So they'd gone their separate ways. If Nancy pre-
ferred a movie to a romantic dinner, that was

her problem. Or at least Jake had tried to tell himself that.

After eating, Jake had headed to the Rock to catch up on research for his poli-sci paper. Bad idea. He could only think of Nancy.

Taking a deep breath, he loped down the steps and began to walk. Maybe the air would clear his head. His gut instincts told him his relationship with Nancy had taken a wrong turn during that crazy long weekend back in River Heights, her hometown.

It should have been a great time. He and her Dad had hit it off. But Nancy had gotten into some off-the-wall fight with Avery, her father's girlfriend. For the life of him, Jake couldn't figure out what had possessed Nancy. Avery was terrific. But the more he told Nancy to try to work it out—for her dad's sake—the more she had given him the cold shoulder.

He couldn't figure it out. Lately he'd even stopped asking what had happened in that department, and Nancy hadn't volunteered information either.

Jake continued on. At the sight of Java Joe's, his spirits rose. He was cold. Hot chocolate would hit the spot. As he approached, he saw the coffee bar had practically cleared out for the evening. Then he spotted a familiar figure in a window seat. "Nancy!" he declared happily. She was smiling, laughing—the best sight he had seen in hours.

So the night wouldn't be a complete washout

after all. Jake had started for the door when he noticed Nancy wasn't alone. Across the table from her, half hidden by a poster tacked to the window, was a guy.

Not just a guy, but Terry Schneider. Man, that Schneider was a real predator. Jake started for the door, then stopped, paralyzed. Nancy bent her head close to Terry's, so close she could easily kiss him. She whispered something. Terry acted startled. Then they both leaned back and laughed and laughed and laughed.

"Jake," Nancy cried as he barged inside. She was happy to see him. But the smile died on her lips at the sight of his face. "What's wrong?"

"Wrong?" Jake's voice was tight.

"Hi, Jake," Terry said. "Want to join us?"

"I'll pass," Jake answered with exaggerated politeness. "Wouldn't want to interrupt a good thing."

The sarcasm in Jake's voice made Nancy cringe. "Hey, Jake," she started, then slowly realized what had happened. "Jake, this is not what you think," she said firmly.

"Oh? And what exactly is it that I'm not supposed to be thinking?" He glared at Terry.

Terry met his gaze without flinching. Then he glanced at Nancy.

Nancy started to answer Jake, but Jake wouldn't let her. His sarcasm exploded into anger. He raised his voice, and the two or three other students seated at the coffee bar turned and stared at Nancy's table.

"No, let's just cut to the chase, Nancy. It's totally clear why you've been so distant lately. Major-league dope that I am, I hadn't figured it out until now. You found a new guy. You've been dating this creep behind my back——"

"Hey, man——" Terry started to protest.

"Forget it. I hope you two enjoy yourselves."

Nancy watched, horrified, as Jake turned and stormed out the door. She stared after him, infuriated.

"What was that about?" Terry exclaimed.

Nancy drew in a deep breath before trusting her voice. "He's got it all wrong," she said tersely.

Terry began to push back his chair. "I'll tell him now, myself. This isn't a date."

"No. Don't do that." Nancy put a restraining hand on his arm. "Terry, this has nothing to do with you, really. Jake and I . . ." Nancy stopped herself before she said something she might regret. "Look, this is between us. I have to sort out exactly what *is* going on here."

Terry looked at Nancy across the table, his expression soft. "If you need to talk or . . ."

"No, Terry. Not now. I think I might just need to be alone."

"I'll walk you back to the dorm."

Nancy considered that a second, then shook her head. "I'd rather stay here awhile."

"Sure?"

"Sure." Nancy was still furious, but she managed to smile at Terry's concern. "Thanks, though."

Terry got up, headed for the door, then turned around. "Call me?"

"I will," she promised, then he left.

The counter person caught Nancy's eye. "Okay?"

"Yeah, I'm okay." Nancy apologized. "Sorry for the scene, though."

"I've seen worse."

Alone, Nancy folded her arms and stared out the window. She took a few deep breaths and tried to calm down.

Nancy was furious at Jake. Still, part of what Jake had said rang true. The part about being distant. Nancy hadn't felt as close to Jake since they'd gotten back from River Heights. He hadn't understood her then. Just like now. Whatever was going on between them, she'd never cheat on him. Even if the relationship wasn't working, she'd try to figure out the reasons why. Try to solve the problems.

At that thought, Nancy bit her lip. Actually she hadn't been trying to solve a thing. She'd been putting off thinking about their relationship. It was all too painful. She loved him. The physical attraction between them was sometimes overwhelming. But she wanted something from Jake that he didn't seem to be giving her. Maybe they just needed a time-out.

Nancy pushed away her half-finished cappuccino. Having a real heart-to-heart with Jake, wherever that might lead, was the only answer to their problems. She owed it to him, and their friendship, to try to work things out.

"Why are Sundays longer than any other day?" Stephanie Keats drummed her fingers against the register behind the cosmetics counter of Berrigan's Department Store. Just one hour into her shift and already Stephanie was aching to leave.

Pam Miller looked up from straightening out the lipstick display. "What we need are some customers."

"What *I* need is a cigarette," Stephanie stated. "Whoever made these idiotic laws about not smoking—"

"Was smart!" Pam cut her off.

"Don't give me your little Miss Surgeon General lecture," Stephanie warned, grabbing a dust cloth and attacking her side of the plate glass counter with a vengeance. "I know it by heart."

"I just can't believe you're this upset about a cigarette," Pam marveled.

"Whatever," Stephanie mumbled, then pursed her lips and turned her back on Pam. When she was sure Pam wasn't looking, she cast a quick glance in the direction of the shipping department. A few minutes ago Jonathan Baur had ducked behind the door. Jonathan wasn't only her manager at Berrigan's, he had been her boyfriend. Not just her boyfriend, she thought bitterly, but the one guy she had ever loved heart and soul.

She'd been so scared of that love, she'd blown it big time. A few days ago he'd found her in her dorm room with another guy. Talk about being dumped on the spot. Well, Stephanie thought now, jamming the lipstick tubes into the Plexiglas display cubbies, I asked for it. But deserving being dropped didn't make it hurt any less.

Now I'll never have to worry about his getting too close to me. Jonathan would be happiest if I were transferred to a department on another planet so he'd never have to see me again.

"Stephanie?"

Stephanie looked up quickly. Pam was frowning.

"Something wrong?"

"No," Stephanie shot back. "Not a thing."

Pam shrugged. "Just asking. You're sort of quiet today."

"Late night last night," Stephanie tossed off.

Pam laughed. "So that's why Jonathan looks kind of spaced."

Stephanie sucked in her breath and turned her back on Pam. Fat chance that Pam or anyone would sympathize if they knew what was really going on.

"I wouldn't know about Jonathan," Stephanie said under her breath. But it was true she hadn't slept a wink since Jonathan had walked out of her life. She wanted—no, she *needed* him back.

She loved him, and somehow she had to get one last chance to prove that to him.

"Stephanie, you really have to be more careful."

"Jonathan," she said, glancing up. As usual, he looked terrific in a well-cut sports jacket, tasteful tie, and dark gray sweater vest. Stephanie offered a tentative smile, but his expression hardened, and her spirits sank. "Now what did I do?"

"You forgot to initial another outgoing order. This carelessness has got to stop."

Jonathan's tone stung her. Stephanie shrank back slightly. "Look, I'm sorry. I've—I've been a bit distracted lately." She lifted her eyes toward his, hoping he'd get the message. Because of you, you dope. You walked out of my life, and I'm falling apart.

Jonathan's dusky gray eyes were cold, and he seemed to look right through her.

Stephanie frowned. "Forgetting to scrawl my S and K on your orders won't make the world stop!"

"*That's* not a very good attitude, Stephanie."

Pam glanced up from fixing the display. "I'm sure Stephanie won't do it again, Jonathan," she said in Stephanie's defense, giving her a puzzled look. "You're being a little hard on her."

Stephanie bristled. She didn't need Pam or anyone to defend her. If Jonathan wanted to act like a jerk, she didn't have to put up with it. She lifted her shoulders in an exaggerated shrug and scoffed. "What else do you expect from Mr. Perfection here? A lower mortal like me just can't manage to live up to his standards." Turning to Jonathan, her voice dripped sarcasm. "Sorry, boss," she drawled. "I won't let you down again."

"Stephanie . . ." Jonathan started to say, raising his voice. Then he threw his hands in the air and stormed off.

"What—" Pam began to ask.

"This is in the mind-your-own-business department, Pam. Get it?"

Pam looked at Stephanie with pity. "Got it," she replied.

CHAPTER 3

Calm down, Drew, Nancy told herself. She stood outside the *Wilder Times* office and forced herself to take ten deep breaths. Last night her decision to seek out Jake first thing and settle whatever was wrong between them made sense. Now in the cold light of day as she pushed open the door to the newspaper office, Nancy felt her courage begin to fail her.

"Hi, Nancy, what's new?" Gary Friedman, the paper's photographer, yelled from a layout table. Other staffers raised their eyes from their work and waved at Nancy.

"Came by to pitch in," Nancy said, scanning the room for Jake. As the office door slammed behind her, Nancy saw Jake duck into the small room that held the photocopier. Nancy swallowed hard. "So you're putting the paper to bed?" she said to Gary with a weak smile. She hung her coat by the door and shoved her bag in a desk drawer.

29

Gary nodded but gave a quick look toward the repro room. "Jake's here," he informed her. He hitched up his baggy pants and yelled over his shoulder, "Collins, look what the wind blew in."

"Ummmm." Jake's mutter was half inaudible.

Nancy's cheeks grew warm as Gary frowned. "What's with him?"

Nancy just shrugged. "So where are we on the layout? What can I do?"

"Better ask Gail," Gary replied, eyeing Nancy curiously.

Nancy went over to the glass-paneled cubicle where the paper's editor, Gail Gardeski, sat. She looked up when Nancy knocked.

"Oh, Nancy, glad to see you. Why don't you proof this last article?" Gail suggested, handing Nancy some copy from her desk. "Just mark the corrections. Gary can key them in later if we need the piece. It's filler, really." Gail got up and followed Nancy out from her cubicle.

They entered the main part of the office, just as Jake stalked out of the repro room. As he passed Nancy, he kept his eyes focused on the floor.

"Jake . . ." Nancy started to say.

Jake cleared his throat and continued toward the coatrack.

"Where are you off to?" Gail asked as Jake grabbed his jacket.

"Just got a lead on a story."

"What story?"

"Trust me, Gail. It's big. I'll let you know when and if it pans out. Gotta run."

Jake banged out the door.

Nancy watched after him, her heart aching.

"What's going on?" Gail asked Nancy quietly.

Nancy hesitated. "I'm not sure," she admitted reluctantly. She found Gail's curiosity a little irritating. "But it's nothing I can't handle." Nancy just hoped she was right.

"Sunday brunch is getting to be a habit with us," Frank Chung said to Ginny Yuen that morning in the Bumblebee Diner.

"I've noticed." Ginny leaned across the table and returned Frank's big sunny smile. "But it's a good habit," she said warmly, and meant it.

"They should consider putting our names on this booth."

Ginny started to laugh. "Now, that's a thought." She loved the corner booth at the diner, and she really had begun to look forward to their weekly brunch date. Since her breakup with Ray, Ginny had grown close to Frank. She had never felt so comfortable with a guy.

Her smile widened at the thought. Frank cocked his head and studied her. For a second Frank tried to hold her gaze, but Ginny looked down quickly at her plate.

Don't mess things up, Frank, she begged him silently. Let's stay just friends. It's easier that way. But the way Frank kept looking at her, she could tell his feelings were more than friendly.

Ginny cleared her throat and checked her watch. "I guess I'd better get going." She looked up at Frank from under her shiny straight bangs. He was handsome, with smooth skin, expressive eyes, and a wonderful smile. He was the kind of guy her parents dreamed of her meeting at college and possibly making a life with. She really did like him, but the problem was, liking Frank didn't compare to what she felt for Ray. Even though she and Ray had been on the outs for some time now, she still loved him truly, madly, deeply.

"I thought you weren't working at the hospital today."

"I'm not." Ginny sighed and reached for Ray's old black leather jacket, the one he had given her before they broke up. She lifted her long hair over the collar and smiled wistfully at Frank. "But I've got a chemistry test coming up and I haven't cracked a book yet. And I promised to spend some time this afternoon tutoring my lab partner, Samantha."

"I hear you. I'm pretty buried myself," Frank said in commiseration. He signaled the waitress for the check. "This one's on me," he told Ginny as she reached for her wallet.

"Thanks, but . . ."

"Come on, Ginny." Frank said. "Even friends treat each other sometime. I'll walk you back to campus. You can catch me up on the latest at Weston General Hospital."

As they strolled back to campus, Ginny relaxed. Talking to Frank about her volunteer work in the pediatrics wing of the hospital always made her happy. Frank seemed genuinely interested in her stories about the kids and their families.

"You know, Ginny," he said as they approached the math and sciences building. "You're going to make one terrific pediatrician."

Ginny laughed. "I don't know about the pediatrician part yet, but I am more and more sure I *am* cut out to be a doctor."

"You are." Frank's tone was firm.

"Of course medical school seems a long way off from where I'm standing, Frank," Ginny said. "But I think if I keep working hard, I'll make the grade."

"But don't work too hard," Frank said, gently brushing her hair back from her face. It was a friendly sort of touch, but Ginny's heart stopped. She wasn't ready for this. At least she didn't think she was. Frank looked as if he was about to bend down and kiss her.

Ginny started up the steps to the building before he had a chance. "I had a really good time today," she said, stopping to turn around. "Thanks again."

"Same time next week?" he said evenly as his eyes registered disappointment.

"Sure," Ginny replied, then began to climb the last few steps. She didn't turn around until she was inside the front door.

Ginny started down the hall toward the reading room. Why did life have to be so complicated?

Why couldn't the guy who set off firecrackers in her soul be the same guy who cared deeply about her career plans?

Ray hadn't been able to fathom why she had to study so much, work so hard, let alone volunteer in the premed hospital program. He just wanted Ginny to be able to spend all her free time with him. Hanging out, writing songs together, making music. He wanted Ginny to be happy, but he was always so involved in his own band that he never remembered to ask how her life was going.

Frank, on the other hand, understood her completely. But he wasn't Ray. Frank was sweet as pie, but he was predictable, steady, with no surprises.

Why couldn't she meet one guy who was different, exciting, offbeat, *and* interested in her career in medicine?

"Dream on!" Ginny murmured as she shouldered her knapsack and wandered into the reading room in search of Samantha, whom she planned to tutor in the intricacies of quantitative analysis.

> TDH—I can't believe how much I love being on-line. Or should I say being *with you* on-line. SSS

Less than twenty-four hours after meeting TDH through the Wilder Usenet, Soozie was back in Graves Hall in front of a terminal, happier than she had been in months. First session on-line, she had met a guy who at least *said* he was tall, dark, and handsome and who was a senior at Wilder. Not bad. Not bad at all.

> SSS—What's not to love about this? TDH
> TDH—If you only knew! SSS
> SSS—Tell me! Tell me! TDH

Here goes nothing! Soozie thought; then remembered that even if she made a fool of herself, who was to know about it? TDH, whoever he was? Feeling free as a bird, she typed the truth.

> TDH—I hated the whole idea of on-line dating. I thought only geeks and nerds wasted time surfing the Net to meet someone. You should have heard me back at my sorority. I really put down one of my sisters for hooking up with some guy—who I admit turned out to be really great—through the chat rooms. I swore I'd never dream of making friends on-line. Do you hate me yet? SSS
> SSS—Hate you? Never. What changed your mind? *Moi*? TDH
> TDH—Hmmm. I'll wait before I answer that. But to tell the truth, this is like writing in a diary. I can just spill out what I want without feeling like anyone is judging me. Because no one knows who I am. Except it's better because this diary talks back! SSS
> SSS—I've been called lots of things in my 21

years but never a diary, let alone a *talking* diary. I wonder if I should be insulted. TDH

TDH—No way. It just feels great not to have to keep up a front. I don't have to look or act any particular way on-line. SSS

SSS—What's wrong with your looks? Blond is good. TDH

TDH—HOW DO YOU KNOW THAT? SSS

Soozie's hand flew to her carefully groomed hair. She checked the terminals near her. Suddenly she felt spied on. But everyone's head was bent over a keyboard or tilted toward the flickering light of a monitor. Then she turned back to the screen.

SSS—Where are you? What's the panic? Blond was just a guess. Oh, and by the way, never use all capital letters on-line. It's sort of like screaming in someone's ear. Shows you're a *newbie*—someone new to the on-line scene. But I know what you mean. I like anonymity, too. At least at first. That way I can let someone in the world out there know the real me. TDH

TDH—Hmmm. I sure can't count you among the clueless nerds on campus. Yes, I am blond. I am in a sorority as I said. And I admit I'm a *newbie.* But what secrets? Come on. I already shared. SSS

SSS—Only fair. Here goes—it's poetry. I write poetry and read it, too. TDH

TDH—Show me—no, *type* me a poem. SSS

SSS—Of mine? Not yet. Not yet. I've never shown anyone my poems, even on-line. TDH

TDH—Don't you trust me? SSS

SSS—Should I? TDH

TDH—Yes. Yes. Yes. SSS

SSS—I'll try. But give me time. Meanwhile, here's a poem I know that sort of says how I'm feeling right now, better than I can myself.

> *I love.* Brave new words.
> New and too soon like daybreak
> after all night with you.
> Not touching yet but oh
> kisses dance across
> all the getting-to-know-you talk.

It hasn't really been all night, but that's how I feel. TDH

Soozie read the poem twice, then touched her lips. She felt as if she'd just been kissed.

Pam Miller peered in the mirror on the door of her locker in the employees' lounge and brushed some blush on her dusky cheeks. "That should do it!" she said to herself, then slammed the locker shut. Humming an upbeat tune, she slung her bag over her shoulder and started for the door.

"Pam?"

"Hi, Jonathan." Pam smiled. "Time to fly the coop."

"Really," Jonathan agreed in a flat voice.

"You could sound a bit more enthusiastic."

Jonathan made a face. "Stephanie around?"

"No. She split as soon as the closing bell rang. She seemed in a rush. Don't know where she went, though, if you're looking for her," Pam added, trying to be helpful.

"I'm not," he stated. He took his coat from his locker and folded it over his arm. "Got a minute?"

"Sure," Pam said, puzzled. "What's up?" she asked, as Jonathan propped himself against one of the lockers.

"Problems in the Stephanie department," he informed her glumly. "You know her as well as anyone does. I need feedback, I guess."

Pam's eyebrows shot up. "Not marking orders really isn't such a big deal."

He looked completely miserable. "I know. I didn't mean to be so tough on her. I'm having a hard time keeping the personal and business stuff separate."

"Makes sense," Pam agreed cautiously.

"Stephanie is not an easy person."

Pam had to laugh. "Even truer." She propped one hip on the arm of the sofa and added gently, "What's going on, Jonathan?"

"I'll spare you the gory details," he said. "Let's just say that I thought she had the same sort of commitment to our relationship that I do. Apparently, she doesn't."

"What does she say?" Pam asked, sure that Stephanie was knock-down crazy over Jonathan.

"That *I'm* the love of her life." Jonathan laughed tightly. "She has a funny way of showing it, though. Pam, what's a relationship about if not trust?"

Now what was Stephanie up to? Pam almost didn't want to know. She certainly didn't want to hear about it from Jonathan. She put up her hand to stop him. "Why are you talking to me about Stephanie? You should talk to her."

"I can't. I'm too angry. Besides, I shouldn't have to spell it all out for her. I'm just not interested in someone I can't trust."

Pam shook her head vehemently. "So tell her that, Jonathan." Thinking about Jamal, her own boyfriend, she added, "Two people have to work out the ground rules of a relationship. You can't expect her to read your mind. No one can do that. And besides," Pam declared, "maybe you're holding Stephanie up to some kind of perfectionist standard that isn't realistic."

Jonathan laughed tightly. "Isn't that what she called me before? Mr. Perfect."

Pam reached out and touched Jonathan's arm. "I didn't mean it that way. But even people we love can have clay feet."

"Maybe so. But I'm not sure I can put up with Stephanie's particular flaws, to be honest with you."

Pam didn't know how to reply to that. She buttoned her coat and said, "Guess I wasn't much help."

"I needed to get it off my chest, Pam. But don't tell Stephanie I talked to you."

"I won't," Pam promised. But as she walked out of the employees' entrance, she felt uneasy. She wished Jonathan hadn't confided in her. Stephanie had told her to mind her own business. Good idea, Pam told herself. The last thing she needed was to get caught in the middle of a messy breakup.

"So, Bess, what's the scoop?" George Fayne asked her cousin Sunday afternoon. George was curled up on one end of Will's couch, half watching Will's roommate, Andy, and his girlfriend, Reva, hard at play in front of a new computer game.

It was a gray, stay-at-home sort of day, and she had a cozy, laid-back Sunday feeling. The week ahead promised no big quizzes, no papers due, and no foreseeable big hassles. "I'm sure you didn't turn up just to sample Will's microwave popcorn," she teased, her brown eyes sparkling.

"Shows what you know." Bess laughed as she hung her bright yellow slicker on a coat hook by the door. George patted the couch, and Bess sat down and sniffed the air.

"Have I got great timing, or what? It smells almost done." She flashed a wicked grin at George. "But I *do* have some major gossip." She kicked off her loafers and curled her feet under her on the couch. "Holly's got a new boyfriend. She brought him around to Kappa last night, and I got to meet him."

"I remember when we saw them hook up for the first time at Java Joe's," George recalled. "So they really are dating now."

"As in he took her to Les Peches," Bess informed her as Will walked in from the kitchen with a bowl of popcorn. Reva and Andy left off their computer game to join the others in front of the crate that served as a coffee table.

"Who took whom to Les Peches?" Andy said.

"Jean-Marc, Holly's new guy. It was their first real date," Bess said, pouring sodas for everyone and handing them around.

Will whistled under his breath. "Pretty impressive for a first date."

Bess giggled. "It impressed a lot of the Kappas. We're all ready to go on-line looking for love."

"If I hadn't already met the best guy in the world, I'd give it a whirl," Reva said. Her black eyes twinkled as she tickled Andy in the ribs.

"Wouldn't that be cool? Let's both go on-line and see if we meet each other all over again," Andy suggested.

"On-line love sounds about my speed these days. Get intimate with some guy you don't have to meet face-to-face. Risk-free relationships."

George flinched at Bess's remark. Bess seemed upbeat and together these days, but George sensed Bess was working a little too hard at acting happy.

"But speaking of Kappas and the Internet," Reva interjected, "George and I were at the computer center earlier and spotted one on the prowl."

"And she sure wasn't doing research," George added with a knowing laugh. "Reva peeked. She was actually in a chat room calling herself SSS."

"SSS?" Bess repeated.

"You'll never guess who it was," George said.

"Haven't a clue," Bess admitted.

"Soozie Beckerman," George and Reva said.

"Hot on the trail of computer love!" George added.

"I don't believe it!" Bess gasped. "But why? She's been putting down the whole idea of online dating ever since she heard Holly was into it."

"Maybe when she met Holly's fabulous Jean-Marc, she got inspired," Will said. "Soozie is competitive if nothing else."

"True," Bess admitted. "But what in the world does SSS mean?"

"Who knows?"

"The person who was in that chat room with her, maybe," Reva suggested.

"You mean she already *met* somebody?" Bess repeated, amazed. "This is big news."

"We don't know that for sure," George cautioned.

"If the guy measures up to Jean-Marc, I'm sure we'll all find out soon enough," Reva remarked.

CHAPTER 4

Casey Fontaine stomped across the small rehearsal room in the Hewlitt Performing Arts Center and planted herself inches from Bess. It was Monday afternoon, and Bess, Casey, and Brian Daglian were midway through an improvisation based on characters Brian had conceived.

Casey poked Bess in the chest. "'Back off, Beth Rose, back off," she said in a menacing tone. "No one messes with Elise Evans's man and lives to brag about it."

Bess tried to react to the fury in Casey's green eyes. Her mouth worked and she burst out laughing.

"Time out!" Casey called, sounding a little annoyed. "Bess, laughter is a pretty weird response."

"I couldn't help it," Bess gasped between giggles. "You looked *so* angry, and I just couldn't get into it," Bess admitted, wiping tears from her eyes. "I wonder if I'll ever get the hang of improv."

"You've more than got the hang of it," Brian assured her. "By the time Jeanne Glasseburg's acting class starts up next semester, you're going to feel really comfortable with these theater exercises. Right, Casey?" He turned to the tall redheaded actress.

"No question," Casey said, adjusting the shoulder strap of her ankle-length jumper. "Bess's work is getting stronger."

Bess heard the note of reserve in Casey's voice. But Brian didn't seem to pick up on it. "See, Marvin, the pro here has confidence in you."

Just then Brian's beeper buzzed. He checked it. "I'm game for another improv, but let me return this call. I think it's my dad."

Bess waited until Brian was safely down the hall, then she said to Casey, "Out with it. Where have I been going wrong?" Bess was determined to prove herself in Glasseburg's class and felt she needed all the coaching she could get. Casey really was a professional, having been a famous teen star in a top-rated TV series. "You're the improv expert!"

"I guess you're too good a friend to fool."

Bess felt a sudden lurch in her stomach. She was sick of her friends always trying to take her emotional temperature. She was just fine. "Why?" Bess laughed. "My cast is off, and I don't even get headaches anymore. The doctor said I am one hundred percent better."

Casey looked up at the ceiling and gave a despairing sigh. "Wrong. The body's better, but the rest of you . . . I sense you're still running away from your real feelings."

"No. I'm not," Bess countered. "I'm still seeing Victoria, my counselor. So I'm facing everything."

Casey started to say more, then bit her lip.

"What's this got to do with acting, anyway?" Bess asked testily.

"Everything. Your performance was good just now, but I don't sense it's coming from the real you. Bess, you're getting pretty terrific at pretending. Pretending you feel okay, that your life is just fine when it isn't."

"I don't do that," Bess denied vehemently.

Casey held her ground. "Yes, you do. And it's affecting your acting. Actors draw from inner experience. Trust me, keeping your personal pain buried is going to trip you up onstage just as in real life, Bess."

Bess sat stunned. Casey's words rang true. But Bess couldn't bear to hear them. The thought of never seeing Paul again made something go cold inside. Bess felt she'd die. She gripped the edge of her chair and managed to shove all the terrible, dark feelings down.

She put on her brightest smile. "Casey Fontaine, you're a piece of work." She got up and looked down at her friend. "Talk about improv. That's a pretty dramatic take on my situation.

Like I said, I've already got a counselor. I'm okay. Really I am. A-okay."

"Okay about what?" Brian asked from the door.

"Casey was just giving me some pointers about acting technique," Bess said airily. Then with forced cheer she added, "I need to grab something from the vending machine." She picked up her bag and smiled broadly at Casey and Brian. "Want anything?" They both shook their heads.

"Back in a sec." Bess flew out of the room with a breezy wave.

But safely out in the theater lobby, she leaned against the wall and burst into uncontrollable sobs.

"Thank goodness he can't see me," Soozie muttered as she punched in her password on the keyboard. She had raced to the computer center right after her European art history class to check her messages from TDH before dashing to Psych 201. Her usually neatly styled hair was windblown, and her shirt was working its way loose from her tailored gray pants. One plus to computer dating was that she could remain anonymous, sight unseen forever if she wanted to.

She hooked in to her E-mail and cheered. "All right, TDH." She had checked twice this morning, and twice there were two new messages. Just as he had promised yesterday. He'd keep checking his mail between classes, and she'd check hers. That way the intense conversation they'd kept up ever since Saturday night could go on, all day, all week, all whatever. Soozie just hoped it would never end.

Now he had replied to her last note, sent late that morning. She read it quickly. He promised to be on-line waiting for her between one forty-five and two that afternoon. That's *now*, Soozie thought, steering herself out of her E-mail and into a chat room.

TDH—I'm here, but I have to rush to class. What's new? I miss you. I miss you. Oh, how I miss you! SSS

   SSS—Miss you, too. More brave new words for you. By the way, I owe them all to the confessional poets. This is by one of the more obscure ones, but I love it.

> Dark cave I walked until you
> Light in love scattered
> Demons of past dreams
> Green fields sprouting roses at your feet
> TDH

TDH—I adore it. Who are these confessional poets? I confess I've never read any poetry except in high school for a lit class, and I never liked it—until now. Maybe it's your special touch? *Your* way with words? You still haven't answered my first question. What *do* you look like? Though I don't know if I care anymore. . . .

Whatever, whoever you are, you're just perfect. SSS

SSS—You make me blush. Like I said, when we meet in person. In fact, I'll tell you *all* about the confessional poets in person. Speaking of meeting in person, when are TDH and SSS going to get together face-to-face? I bet you have the bluest eyes. But like you said, whatever, I really, really am enjoying learning all about you. TDH

He's asking me on a date! Soozie couldn't believe it. Now he's even figured out I've got blue eyes. Fate. Pure fate! She leaned in toward the screen and grinned until her face hurt. She and TDH had begun their on-line relationship only a couple of days ago, and already he was ready to meet her.

Then a little warning bell went off in Soozie's head. Was she moving too fast? As she had warned Holly about only a few weeks back, you never could tell who or *what* you might meet online. Suzie hesitated, then smiled. That was the fun of it. Besides, no one too terrible could lurk on Wilder's Usenet. Hadn't Holly found Jean-Marc there? This was the chance of a lifetime, and she had to take it.

The campus clock chimed two. Quickly she typed her reply.

TDH—I'm game. I already feel like I know so much about you, but I need to know more. To

see you in person to . . . well, I won't say here,
but post the time and place. I'll check back later.
Gotta go to class. . . . SSS

Nancy peered in the window of the small coffee shop on the corner of College Avenue and
Main. Terry had already arrived and was sitting
with a cup of coffee in a corner booth, reading a
book. Before she walked through the door, she
checked once over her shoulder. Jake was supposed to be in class right now, but she couldn't
risk his running into her with Terry. Not after
the scene Jake had made on Saturday.

As Nancy approached the booth, Terry
looked up.

"I was beginning to think I had the wrong
place," he said, closing his book.

"Sorry I'm late," Nancy apologized. "I had to
wait to talk to Professor Bates after western civ
about my next paper." She took off her coat and
sat across from him. "Thanks for meeting me
here on such short notice," she said, signaling the
waitress to order a cup of coffee.

"Like I said when you phoned, I was really
glad to hear from you. If I didn't run into you
soon, I was going to call."

"Well, I *have* been better," Nancy admitted
with a small frown. A second later she shook it
off and smiled at Terry. "Look, I asked if you
could meet me so that I could apologize to you
in person. Jake was pretty outrageous, and I'm
sorry you landed in the middle of it."

"No need. Stuff happens. That's what makes life interesting," Terry said.

"I'll take mine dull, thank you," she said, and stirred some sugar into her coffee.

"So did Jake cool off the other night?"

"I wouldn't know," Nancy said. Jake had avoided her for two whole days, since Sunday at the *Times* office. He hadn't returned one of her calls.

"Nancy, I can be a good listener if you want to talk about it," Terry said.

Nancy thought a moment. It might be good to have a guy's take on the situation.

"I'm not sure what there is to talk about," she finally said. "Jake seems to have slammed the door in my face. He won't give me a chance to explain."

"He was pretty freaked out," Terry said.

"So am I, Terry," Nancy responded a little hotly. "I thought I knew him. And I hoped he *knew* me. I wouldn't two-time him," she said. "I wouldn't two-time anyone, ever."

"I believe that," Terry said, "but jealousy blinds people. Jake's probably scared he's losing you."

Nancy stared bleakly at Terry, and her anger went up like smoke. "I know," she said, toying with her napkin. After a second she continued, "I'm a very confused freshman right now."

"Ah, and you want advice from a mature, wise upperclassman." Terry leaned back and grinned at Nancy. His eyes were kind and full of concern.

Nancy began to smile. "Wise . . . okay. But mature?" she teased him, then instantly grew serious. "But, yes. Where to begin?" She sipped some coffee and cleared her throat. "You know that before I met Jake, I'd been involved with another guy for a long time."

"This is the guy at Emerson, right?"

Nancy nodded. "We dated through high school, and when he went to college, we stayed together. We're still friends, by the way," Nancy added. "Anyway, I met Jake not long after Ned and I broke up. I'm sort of wondering if I was crazy to jump into a major-league relationship so fast."

"On the rebound," Terry stated.

"Right. And maybe that's what's wrong. Maybe I never sorted out my feelings about Ned first. Jake was right there, and so attractive. I thought it would be casual, and I tried to keep it that way. But believe me, it's anything but casual," Nancy confessed. Just the thought of Jake made her go into major meltdown. Something must still be *right* between them.

"Nancy, I figured from the get-go that you and Jake weren't a casual item. Just like I sort of figured you're not a very casual person."

She looked up quickly. "But that's the point. Maybe for once I *want* to be a casual person. I've gone right from one intense relationship to another. Maybe it's too much, too soon. I just want to have fun, meet new people, try new things."

"Nan, maybe you and Jake just need some downtime. Maybe you need to talk it out between the two of you. He'll cool off. The guy's probably confused and embarrassed. Jake seems to really care for you. Anyway, I'm sure you can work this out yourself. Just listen to your heart. You know how I feel about you. I'm rooting for you to be a free single person again. It's hard to be impartial here. Still, whatever works out for you, whatever makes you happy, I'll be your friend."

Nancy felt like kissing Terry for that. Bad idea. Still, part of her was flattered that he found her attractive. "What can I say?" Nancy sat back and smiled at him. "Thanks for promising to be there for me, whatever happens."

As they paid for their coffee and headed their separate ways, Nancy realized again how much Terry reminded her of the good, strong parts of Ned and how much Jake didn't.

Nancy crossed the sun-drenched campus, her mind full of Ned, then Terry, then Jake. By the time she reached her suite in Thayer Hall, Nancy was more confused than ever and feeling just a little bit guilty. Confiding in Terry had felt like betraying Jake, the guy she really loved. The guy she *thought* she loved.

Holly Thornton sat in the sunroom, just off the side porch of Kappa house, watching *After Midnight,* her favorite daytime drama, with Jean-Marc on one side of her, a box of tissues on the

other. Holly adored soap operas, and she was beginning to more than adore Jean-Marc. She'd
been seeing him for only about a week, but she
was falling head-over-heels in love.

"I love soap operas," Jean-Marc declared as a
commercial blipped on the TV screen. He zapped
it with the remote and wound his fingers in Holly's wavy hair. Holly lifted her face to his for a
quick kiss. She melted against him and wished
they were somewhere more private.

Light, airy, and filled with lush green and
flowering plants, the sunroom was almost every
Kappa's favorite spot. Darcy was on a treadmill
in the corner near the door. Marsha Nelson,
Chris Murphy, and some other sisters were at a
long mahogany table near the wall, working on
a collaborative project for their senior media
studies seminar.

"Hi, guys," Leila said as she walked in the
room with Janie just behind her and dumped an
armful of shopping bags on a chair. "Janie just
took me shopping." Turning to Darcy, she continued, "You should check out Play It Again, that
retro clothing store. I found a fab outfit for that
voice department concert I'm giving next week."

"Sometimes I think secondhand's the only way
to shop," Janie said. "But don't tell Soozie I
said so."

"Why not?" Jean-Marc asked. "The retro
look's really hot back home in Quebec."

"Retro is not considered good Kappa form—
at least according to Soozie's standards," Holly

said. "She's always after Janie to change her look."

Jean-Marc made a face. "Isn't Soozie the girl who put down on-line dating?"

"The same."

"She's going to wish she didn't!" Bess declared, entering the room, Casey in tow.

"Hi, Bess, Casey," Holly said.

"So what's the Sooze up to now?" Janie asked.

"She's hooked up with some guy on-line," Bess informed the room.

"Get out!" Darcy exclaimed, from the treadmill.

Marsha Nelson commented, "She's got nerve if nothing else."

"After the way she put down meeting people on-line, I can't believe it," Chris Murphy said with a giggle.

"Really," Holly said, not sure whether she felt annoyed or amused. "Soozie swore up and down that only nerds need to find dates on-line."

"I guess that makes Soozie a nerd," Janie said tartly.

Holly chuckled. "I wouldn't blame you for teasing her about it. She deserves it. Kind of gives you a chance to get back at her for all the mean stuff she's done to you over the years."

"What stuff?" Bess asked.

"Oh, nothing," Janie brushed off Holly's remark.

"Nothing?" Holly couldn't believe her ears. "Come off it. You two have some heavy back

history in this house." Turning to Bess, Holly elaborated. "Soozie has pulled some pretty nasty tricks on Janie over the years."

"Look, that's old news." Janie acted embarrassed and toyed with the neckline of her embroidered shirt.

"I wouldn't get over it that easily," Leila said.

"Over *what?*" Bess demanded.

"Soozie actually threw out *all* of Janie's clothes one night when Janie was crashing at a friend's apartment. She said Janie didn't have the right Kappa look!" Holly said.

Bess gasped. *"Unbelievable!"*

Jean-Marc frowned. "That makes no sense. Was there a reason?"

"There was," Darcy said, defending her. "Soozie headed a committee to set a Kappa dress code." With an apologetic look at Janie, Darcy added, "Janie balked—"

"Lots of girls did; that's why it didn't go through," Holly reminded her.

"True, but Soozie thought Janie was behind the vote against the code. So she took it out on Janie."

"But Janie wasn't even here the week we voted," Leila pointed out.

"She's just never liked me," Janie said. "You're making too much of it."

"I don't know about that," Jean-Marc commented. "But Soozie had better be careful. If she keeps being mean to people, she's going to make enemies. That's no fun."

"True," Holly said, then turned to Bess. "Finally, things got so bad when Soozie set up this really terrible blind date for Janie—" Holly caught Janie's eye. "Okay, I'll spare everyone the details of that episode. But the upshot was that the two of them couldn't both live here."

"'So you moved out?" Bess looked at Janie.

"It wasn't such a big deal. I'm a senior. It's my last year here. Besides, as I told you before, I like living on my own."

"I can't believe you aren't still upset about this," Bess said.

"She is," Holly said softly.

But Janie overheard. "Not really. I like having my own place," she declared.

Just then the porch door flew open and Soozie breezed in, whistling. "Hi, gang," she said, and hung her scarf and coat on the tall oak rack by the door.

The girls exchanged glances, and Holly barely smothered a giggle. Under her breath, she told Jean-Marc, "This should be fun!"

Bess cleared her throat. "So, SSS, what's new?"

Holly watched the pink in Soozie's cheeks deepen to crimson. "SSS," Soozie repeated. "What do you mean by that?"

"It's your handle, isn't it?" Casey remarked in an innocent voice. "Or did I get that wrong, Bess?"

Bess's blue eyes grew wide. "Oh, I don't think

so. Everyone's talking about how SSS has just hit the Internet, big time."

"SSS?" Leila put her finger on her chin and looked thoughtful. "Let me see. Slim Slinky Soozie?"

Janie cracked up.

"Haven't you guys got anything better to do with your lives than nose around in other people's business?" Soozie gave Bess a dirty look. "But if you have to know, it's Stylish Sister Soozie!"

"Always good to know someone who thinks so well of herself," Holly said teasingly.

Darcy chuckled. "What's *the guy's* handle?"

"TDH!" Soozie replied smugly. "And we've already made a date to meet *off-line* in person."

"That's fast," Holly commented. "What does *TDH* stand for?"

"Wouldn't you like to know," Soozie said.

"Go ahead, make my day," Janie remarked.

"TDH—The Dream Hunk?" Bess ventured.

"Tall, Dark, Handsome," Soozie replied with a self-satisfied smile.

Casey threw her head back and laughed. "Of course. Tall, dark, handsome. You're made for each other."

Jean-Marc nodded vigorously. "I told you. It's the perfect place to meet the perfect person. It worked for us," he said, gazing at Holly. "Maybe it will work for Soozie. I hope it does."

"Well, thanks. I hope so, too," Soozie said, blushing prettily.

"That's more like it," Holly said, still feeling a little irritated with Soozie but mainly curious as to what her on-line hunk would be like. "Glad you've seen the light—or screen, as the case may be."

"Everyone's entitled to be wrong at least once in her life," Soozie said, and plopped down on the sofa next to Bess. "I was wrong about the on-line thing. It *is* fun. I went into a chat room and, violà, there he was, the guy of my dreams."

"Or nightmares," Janie suggested.

"You're just jealous," Soozie taunted.

"No." Janie shrugged. "But I seem to remember you're the one who told Holly that meeting some guy in person that you'd chatted up on the Net could be asking for trouble. You never know who lurks out there." Janie hummed a few bars of a spooky tune from a TV horror series.

"You just can't stand to see another person happy," Soozie said hotly.

But Janie continued to press her. "Hasn't it occurred to you that this guy might be some kind of weirdo?"

"Of course not," Soozie answered testily, but she shivered in spite of herself.

CHAPTER 5

"Here you are," George announced. "Haven't seen you in a while, Nan. Thought I'd drop by."

"Hey, George, you *are* a sight for sore eyes," Nancy said.

"I was about to leave here and drop by Jake's place on my way to dinner with Will. I figured you'd be there, studying or *whatever*," George said, emphasizing the last word with a knowing smile. "We thought we could interest you two in sharing a pizza."

Nancy's stomach clenched. "Well, you won't find me at Jake's, that's for sure," Nancy said, then tossed her books on the table.

"Why not?" George asked, startled.

"Because it looks like we broke up," Nancy stated flatly.

"What happened?" George wanted to know.

"I don't know," Nancy said, then asked George to sit down so she could tell her about

Saturday night and the scene at Java Joe's. "He's been avoiding me ever since. He's wrong about Terry . . . and—"

George interrupted angrily. "You'd never cheat on anyone, Nancy."

Nancy laughed. "Thanks for the vote of confidence. Not that Terry would mind. He's had a thing for me ever since we met. And I have to admit I do think he's cute." Nancy hesitated, then finally blurted out, "Oh, George, he reminds me so much of Ned."

George's jaw dropped. "Wow. Now that you bring it up, he *could* be Ned's double."

"Not just in looks, either," Nancy added. "He's easy to talk to. I don't feel like I'm sparring with him all the time. Just now, over coffee, he was pretty helpful. He gave me a guy's point of view." Nancy laughed. "He understands me, without my having to explain what's going on in my head—as opposed to Jake these days." Nancy got up and restlessly paced. "Sometimes I think Jake and I come from different planets. I never had these kinds of problems with Ned."

"It wasn't always smooth sailing," George reminded Nancy. "I think you might be over-romanticizing what went on between you two."

Nancy disagreed. "No. Our problems didn't start until I came to college. Maybe that's the problem—coming to college. Everything's been changing so fast since I got here in September." Nancy thought of the changes back home: Avery, her dad, losing Ned. Suddenly being on her own in a brand-new life didn't feel so terrific.

"All relationships go through rocky patches," Dawn pointed out.

"Maybe so," Nancy conceded, and wondered for a moment if Ned and she might have weathered *their* latest rough patch had she tried to stick it out.

Nancy bit her lip and pushed memories of Ned aside. Their relationship was past tense by now. But she did need someone to understand her the way Ned always had. As strongly as she felt for Jake, she was beginning to question if he fit the bill.

Grinning at the computer screen, Soozie felt like a fool. She tried to hide her face behind the wall of the cubicle in the computer lab so none of the other students surfing the net could see her.

TDH was making her act perfectly silly. She had dressed up for this last computer-only on-line date, as if he could actually see her through some kind of video telephone. She had tied her hair up in a high ponytail and was wearing a blue silk shirt and slim black jumper.

She called up her E-mail box and practically cheered. TDH had posted a message for her. He was probably suggesting where and when to meet face-to-face. She pointed and clicked on Retrieve and called up TDH's message. As she read, her smile dimmed.

SSS—Forget The Underground. It's too crowded. I want to be alone . . . with you. How about by the lake? The moon is full . . . nothing to distract us from US. The time for talking has ended. Confirm in our chat room at 4 p.m. Oh, hon, don't keep me waiting. I can't bear this suspense a second longer. TDH

"Hon?" Soozie murmured. How tacky! TDH had never said *that* before. She leaped into the screen and read the note again, just to be sure. Where was the poetry? What was TDH up to? And the part about time for talking being over— Soozie *loved* talking to this guy. And what was all this stuff about being alone? By the lake. Soozie frowned.

What had Janie said the other night? That her dream guy might be a nightmare. Maybe everything here *was* moving too fast. Soozie made a quick decision. She exited her E-mail and headed for the on-line chat room.

Sure enough, TDH was there. Before she could change her mind, she began to type.

TDH—The date's off. Too much too soon. I like the slow-and-easy getting to know you on-line. And I love *talking*. SSS

SSS—After all we've shared, I'm surprised at you. You aren't afraid, are you? Though, come to think of it, scary can be fun! Picture the two of us alone under the full moon. Mmmmm. You would look beautiful scared. TDH

Soozie gaped at the message in dismay. After only a second, she flipped the machine off. Her heart pounding, she grabbed her books and jacket and half ran down the aisle of the lab. Head down, she bolted up the steps and slammed into Nick O'Donnell.

"Whoa!" he cried, grabbing her by her arms. "What's with you? You look like you've seen a ghost."

"Oh, please, please, get out of my way," Soozie cried, and twisted out of his grasp.

Nick stepped back. "Hey, you're really scared. What happened?" he asked, concerned.

"None of your business," Soozie said, squeezing by him. Then she saw the worry in his face. He might be a nerd, but he was a nice one. She swallowed hard. "Sorry. But I just need to get out of here."

"Why?"

"I don't want to talk about it. But you won't be seeing me within ten miles of here again."

Nick pressed back against the wall to let her pass. "I thought you were into some hot and heavy on-line relationship," he said, sounding puzzled.

"What's it to you?" she snapped, then saw the hurt in Nick's eyes. "I'm sorry. I've just had some bad news on-line. Not that it matters now. I'm finished with chat rooms. And not a second too soon."

"Stephanie Keats, unglue yourself from that mirror!" Pam urged from the door of Stephanie's room in Suite 301, Thayer Hall. Stephanie continued to tweeze her eyebrows.

"You already look drop-dead beautiful, and we're late for our shift," Pam continued impatiently.

Casey glanced up from her desk, surprised. "You're working this afternoon? You'd better lose those jeans and grab a skirt and get out of here."

"To work or not to work. That's the question." Stephanie strolled with deliberate slowness over to her bed. She was wearing tight jeans and a top that showed her toned midriff. "I dimly recall life before Kiki, when I didn't *have* to work to survive. Do you think my dad's divorced her yet? Do you think I'll get my credit cards back? Will I ever be transformed from shopkeeper to shopper?"

"That's pretty vile, Stephanie," Casey remarked, surprised. "You haven't been that hard on Kiki in weeks. What's with her?" she asked Pam.

"She's either trying to single-handedly change Berrigan's no-jeans dress code—a cause I totally support—or she's looking to get fired."

"Fired. Now there's an idea." The thought that Jonathan might actually fire her made her so upset she reached for her cigarettes. She put one in her mouth before she caught Pam's warning glance and jammed it back in the pack.

"Stephanie fired?" Casey laughed. "Not as long as Jonathan Baur is her manager."

"Wrong," Stephanie said in contradiction. "It would give Jonathan the greatest pleasure to fire me."

"Run that by me again?" Casey said, astonished.

"Jonathan's been a little hard on Stephanie lately," Pam said quietly.

"Not that I don't deserve it," Stephanie blurted out, then folded her arms across her chest. She stared bleakly at Casey. "Go on. Say it."

"Say what?" Casey asked.

" 'I told you so,' because you did. You warned me that I'd better clean up my act." Stephanie broke off and glanced quickly at Pam. Pam didn't need to know *everything*. About how Jonathan had found another guy walking out of her room one morning. The hurt and dismay on Jonathan's face had been so awful, Stephanie would never forget it. She pulled out her last cigarette and lit it.

She shook her hair back from her face and stared, tight-lipped, out the window. "I've really blown it," she said without turning around. "You told me Jonathan wouldn't put up with my—my flirting . . ." she said for Pam's sake, but Casey's eyebrows shot up. Casey knew perfectly well Stephanie hadn't been just flirting with other guys. "You were right. He dumped me."

Stephanie caught Pam's eye, and Pam quickly shifted her gaze. "Not quite true, is it, Pam?" Stephanie said sarcastically. "He actually is talking to me—every chance he gets—to put me down. He doesn't care now what happens between us. Pam can fill you in on those gory details."

Pam cleared her throat. "But he does care."

Stephanie's head snapped up. "How do you know?"

Pam tossed her bag on Stephanie's bed. "Jonathan more or less said so."

Stephanie eyed Pam shrewdly. "Have you two been talking about me behind my back?"

"Cool it, Stephanie," Pam ordered. "It wasn't like that. Jonathan made me swear I wouldn't tell you what he said. But Sunday, after work, he was moping around the locker room.

"Moping? That's a good sign," Stephanie said, a glint in her eye. "It means he actually *might* still care. Now, what did he say—word for word?"

Pam conveyed the gist of her conversation with Jonathan, then said, "It seems he wants some sort of commitment from you."

"I may not be a Girl Scout, Pam, but I am committed. I'm just new at this commitment routine." Stephanie sat heavily at the foot of her bed, then frowned. "Hey, why isn't he telling me this himself? Why's he talking to you? I've got ears."

"Apparently not big enough to hear him with," Casey joked. "And it seems, last I remember, he did try to talk to you about your—*flirting.*" Casey added with a wicked grin. "Didn't do much good, did it?"

Stephanie balled up a piece of paper and tossed it at Casey. "So I'm not perfect!"

"I told him he was too hard on you," Pam said, "and that he should be talking to you, not me. But he feels you should understand where he's coming from without his having to spell it all out for you," she added gently.

Stephanie looked from Pam to Casey. "I just give up. Maybe I'm not cut out for love."

"Yeah, right!" Casey and Pam both said simultaneously.

"Okay, who am I kidding? I do love the guy. But I also love being the object of every cute hunk's attentions. How do you do it, Casey? Guys notice you all the time, but you turn them down. Even though Charley is miles away and wouldn't have a clue if you cheated on him."

'I think he *would* know," Casey said thoughtfully. "But believe me, it's not easy being engaged to someone. Ever since he gave me this ring, I seem to have developed radar to detect every guy who's a perfect ten on campus."

"So how do you deal with it?" Pam asked.

"It's hard. But I keep reminding myself that with Charley I've got something special, something different. We're on the same wavelength—" Casey broke off. "I can't put it in words exactly, but he seems to see right into my soul. Other guys don't—they only see the red hair, the fact I've been a TV star. The glamorous me!" Casey faked a snobbish accent.

Stephanie and Pam cracked up.

A moment later Pam said, "Jonathan and you have the same sort of thing, Stephanie. I think he loves the real you. Not just your sexy image."

"What's wrong with my image?" Stephanie pretended to look offended, but her heart thrilled to Pam's words. Somehow she knew they were true. "But what can I do about this 'real love' for the 'real me,' when he won't give either 'me' another chance?"

"Maybe he will," Casey suggested.

"He will?" Stephanie's hopes began to stir. "What makes you say that? How can I convince him I've changed? Besides," she said, her heart sinking again, "he wants too much."

"What do *you* want?"

Stephanie stared at Casey. "Jonathan."

"Good answer!" Pam said in congratulation.

"Then you'll have him," Casey declared.

"But how, Casey? Short of kidnapping him from the locker room and dragging him off in handcuffs, I can't quite picture how I'll get a chance to convince him to let me explain myself."

"Let's not worry about what *he'll* let you do," Casey said. "If you want him, we'll come up with a plan to make that happen."

Stephanie noted the glee in Casey's voice. She began to smile. "You mean it!"

"I do."

"Trust Casey to be creative." Pam chuckled. "I can't wait to see what she comes up with."

"Same here!" Stephanie cheered. She looked at her watch, peeled off her jeans, and tossed her top onto a chair. "Pam, give me five and I'll be ready for work. This girl's not ready to quit just yet—Berrigan's *or* Jonathan."

The click of heels across the bare wood floor of Radical Moves' rehearsal loft made Ray look up. "Montana, what brings you here?" He handed Cory the sheet of lyrics as he strode toward Montana.

"Just checking up on you guys," Montana replied, flipping her thick mane of curls back from her face. Ray breathed in the fresh, flowery fragrance of Montana's perfume. He couldn't help but think that if and when he ever was ready for someone other than Ginny, Montana would be the one. She was tall, beautiful, and bubbly, and he loved those cool pointy-toed cowboy boots. Plus, she always made him laugh.

She'd made it perfectly clear she was available. But even if Ginny and he really were through, he still couldn't imagine dating anyone else. By the time he'd be ready for romance, a beauty like Montana would probably be hooked up with another guy.

"So did you come to join the party or what?" Karin asked with fake brightness.

The edge of sarcasm in Karin's voice went over Montana's head. "Actually I'm here on business." She took off her fringed suede jacket, sat down, and pulled a datebook out of her bag. She directed her remarks to Ray. "Kara, Nikki, and I were brainstorming yesterday about ideas for our radio show. I thought how cool it would be to interview you, Ray. Your fans are wondering what you've been up to."

"Come off it," Ray protested. He shot a sheepish glance at the others.

Austin was eyeing Montana skeptically. Cory looked about ready to get sick. Montana made no secret she was interested in Ray.

"No kidding. Anyway, I think we could do a straight interview, where you tell us about your band, how it feels working with new people, how you get your sound together . . ."

"Montana," Ray said firmly. "Radical Moves is a joint venture. Interview the whole band, or none of us."

"I'd go for that," Montana said enthusiastically.

"Count me out," Austin said sharply.

"Why?" Montana asked.

"I don't do interviews," Austin said, and grabbing his guitar, he turned his back on the conversation and began running through a riff.

"Cory?"

"I'll do it," Karin suddenly spoke up. "In fact, I think it would be much more fun to have a woman band member together with a guy. Fans always wonder about personal relationships in a band."

Austin's fingers fumbled over his chords, making a jarring sound. Ray winced.

"The whole guy-girl relationship angle should really grab your listeners," Karin added.

"Guy-girl angle?" Montana sounded dismayed. Ray watched as Montana's expression slowly shifted from hurt to resignation. "Oh, I guess Karin's got a point. Let's go for it, you two. You can sing something bluesy and soulful to Ray's guitar accompaniment. Your voices," Montana added ruefully, "are made for each other."

"Now, this should be fun, right, Ray?" Karin put one hand on his shoulder and leaned against him.

He sidled away, with a quick glance in Austin's direction. Austin was curled over his guitar, strumming a series of dissonant, angry chords. Ray blew out his breath. He felt cornered. Reluctantly he said, "Uh, sure. Whatever you say. Just pick a time and place. I'll be there."

And he would—not that he'd have to love it. He was beginning to wonder if Radical Moves had a chance of surviving both Karin *and* Montana.

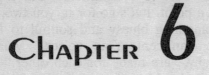

CHAPTER 6

Brrring, brrring, brrring.

"Somebody'd better get that phone," Holly muttered late Tuesday night. She checked the time on her alarm clock and groaned. Three A.M. Not late Tuesday night—early, as in *very* early Wednesday morning. She yanked her comforter over her head, and jammed her hands over her ears. *"I'm* not answering it again," she grumbled into her pillow.

Holly's room was at the top of the stairs, right next to the public house phone. She was usually happy to pick up whenever she was in her room. But this was beginning to get annoying. The phone had been ringing all night, but whenever she answered it, no one was there. *Annoying* was the least of it. Holly had a heavy schedule Wednesday, and it looked as if she'd have to face it without sleep.

The phone continued to ring. Finally Holly

heard a door creak open. Someone padded down the hall, then picked up the receiver. "Hello?" The voice paused and repeated. "Hello? Hello?" Another pause, then Holly heard the hang-up.

"No one's there," the voice whispered, sounding vexed.

"Can't we do something about it?" another voice asked. Holly thought she recognized Darcy.

"Unplug the phone," the first voice suggested.

"We can't. It's fixed into the wall. Maybe we can call the phone company to disconnect it if this keeps up," Darcy said. "Or at least have them trace these calls. This is getting creepy."

Holly flopped back down in her bed and shook her head. Whatever was going on was making every Kappa who lived in the house perfectly miserable.

Holly rolled over on her side. She closed her eyes. Just as she began to drift off to sleep, the ringing started again. This was getting more than annoying. As Darcy had said, it was getting creepy.

Soozie sat scrunched in a corner of her bed. Just when she thought the phone had stopped ringing for good, it started again. This time somebody other than Holly answered it.

Again, no one was there.

Soozie tugged down the hem of her silk nightshirt and tucked her toes under her blankets. In spite of the heat in her room, she felt a chill course up her spine. The phone ringing constantly was beginning to unnerve her, and Soozie's nerves were already frazzled.

"I bet you look beautiful when you're scared . . ." She could picture the words on the screen now.

TDH. Tall, Dark, Handsome—and weird?

Soozie couldn't believe it. How could someone who sent her such sweet notes, who seemed like a soulmate, suddenly turn so twisted?

She had broken down and checked her E-mail again just after dinner, and again after cappuccino with friends at Java Joe's. There were three notes posted. One of them was sweet as springtime. TDH wondered why she had dropped him. He begged her to reconsider their date.

Then the two other notes. They were disgusting. Soozie didn't even want to think about them. The tone was taunting, prodding. Insulting, too, calling her "babe," and "hon," and all sorts of overly familiar names. Ugh. If TDH were trying to scare her off, he was doing a pretty good job.

Soozie looked at the clock. It was almost 4 A.M. The phone had been quiet for nearly a half-hour now. Maybe it would all stop. Maybe she and everyone else could get some rest.

She began to slide beneath the sheets when it started again. "Give me a break!" Soozie cried, unable to stand it. She jumped out of bed and raced from her room without bothering to grab her robe. The phone was down at the end of the hall, by the top of the steps, near Holly Thornton's room.

"Hello!" Soozie shouted into the receiver.

Nothing. Not a sound.

"Whoever you are, you'd better stop it now!" she practically screamed, clutching the receiver with both hands.

"Stop it!" she cried, and slammed down the phone. Shaking from head to toe, she ran back to her room. Safely inside, she leaned against the door, trying to catch her breath.

Suddenly an awful thought occurred to her. The phone calls had begun tonight, after she had ignored TDH's latest on-line messages.

"No!" she said out loud. No way. TDH didn't know who she was, where to find her. Or did he?

Soozie sank down on her bed and forced her mind to slow down. Mentally, she reviewed each on-line conversation—she knew each one by heart. What had she told this guy? That she was a junior at Wilder, that she was in a sorority. But she hadn't said which one. Or not exactly. She *had* mentioned being into the arts and wanting to go into arts administration.

Kappa was the art sorority on campus.

It wouldn't take an Einstein to figure out she was a Kappa sister.

And TDH, a literary guy who was into poetry and computers, was probably no slouch in the brains department.

"What have I done?" Soozie cried, as the hall phone began to ring and ring and ring.

Jake sat alone in his apartment, brooding.

It was not a brooding sort of day. The sun was

bright, the air was clear, and his roommates were somewhere else. Jake didn't know and didn't care where.

Usually he savored the time alone in his apartment. Sometimes, like now, he'd even turn off the tape deck and bask in a rare moment of quiet. He had uncanny powers of concentration and in two hours, without interruption, he could finish a twenty-page paper or write up that week's *Wilder Times* assignment or barrel through the homework that had piled up while he'd been off scooping out a story.

That afternoon, as he sat at his desk, his brain felt like a jumble of wires, all color coded but disconnected and useless.

He shoved his chair back and started for the fridge for a soda. The phone by his bed began to ring.

He let it ring: once, twice, three times. Then the machine clicked on and his taped message played.

"You just missed the one and only Jake Collins. Don't make me miss you. Leave a message at the tone. Catch up with you soon."

"Jake?" This time the sound of Nancy's voice didn't make him mad.

"Hey," she continued, "I know you're there. If you don't pick up in exactly three seconds, I'm calling Missing Persons. One . . . two . . ."

Before Jake had a chance to change his mind, he bolted for the bedside table and yanked up the receiver.

"Nancy. I'm here."

"Knew it!" She gave a triumphant little laugh, but behind the laugh he heard how nervous she sounded.

He'd been avoiding her for days. Now he was so glad to hear from her. "What's up?"

Nancy laughed into the phone. "Shouldn't I be the one asking that?"

Jake leaned back against the wall and cracked a smile. "Touché."

"You've been avoiding me," she said.

Trust Nancy to be direct.

"I just needed time to cool down, Nancy. I was really freaked the other night." He tried to force down the vision of her in Java Joe's leaning so close to that Schneider creep.

"To put it mildly," Nancy said a little more lightly. "And there was no reason to be, Jake. Really."

Nancy was telling the truth. He could hear it in her voice. "That makes me feel pretty stupid," he said with the smallest of smiles.

"In this case, for such a smart guy, you are, or were"—Nancy's laugh was self-conscious—"well, you said it first—stupid." Suddenly Jake pictured her. The way her strong mouth went soft just before they kissed; her blue eyes, so determined, shrewd, kind, and beautiful all at once. The curve of her jaw, the feel of her skin. More than that, her honesty and humor. How could he have doubted her?

"I love you, Nancy," he blurted out.

"I love you, too." Nancy's reply was instant, but he heard her holding back. "But we've got problems. And Terry is *not* one of them."

"I hear you," Jake said, stretching out on his bed and closing his eyes. "We've got to talk."

"I—I feel that by now you should know me better," Nancy said.

"What do you mean?"

"Thinking I'd cheat on you, for one thing."

"Can't blame me for that. You're incredible. And I don't just mean your looks, Nan. You're the most terrific woman I've ever met. I don't want to lose you to some guy who senses we're going through a rough time."

Nancy laughed, a warm, full laugh that gave Jake hope. "Thanks for the compliment—I think."

"But I admit I was wrong. I overreacted with Terry. I apologize," he said, sitting up.

"Apology accepted." Nancy sounded immensely relieved.

Jake suddenly felt lighter, happier than he had in days.

"But you were right about my being more distant with you. Something's going on with us, and we've got to work it out, Jake."

Jake's spirits fell. "I know that."

"I don't know what's gotten into you. It's like you don't know me anymore. You don't understand me."

"I'm trying, Nancy," Jake said, frowning. "But you're making it very hard."

"I'm making it hard?" Nancy suddenly sounded frustrated. "I'm trying to patch things up here."

Jake fell silent. "I'm not sure exactly what needs patching up," he said. "But I have my own take on this. I need to talk to you about something important, Nancy, if you'll hear me."

"I'm listening."

Jake shook his head. "No. Not over the phone."

"Jake, let's not put this off any longer," Nancy said impatiently. "I told you what's bothering me. It's your turn." She paused. "Besides, when we're together we sort of get distracted from *talking.*"

"Hmmm, I've noticed," Jake replied softly. He forced his mind off to the wonderful thought of holding Nancy in his arms. He cleared his throat and said firmly, "I'm serious. Let's get together and just talk. Face-to-face."

Nancy gave a frustrated sigh. "Okay. When?"

"As soon as possible," Jake said, forcing back the uneasy feeling in his gut.

"Let me think," Nancy said. "Tonight—"

"Not tonight," Jake said. "I don't want this to be a date."

"Okay. Then tomorrow. Early. Kara has an early class, so why don't you come over here to Thayer."

"Good," Jake said, trying to sound enthusiastic. "Tomorrow then?"

"Tomorrow," Nancy said, immensely relieved. Jake hung up and his heart sank. He didn't relish what he had to say to Nancy *or* look forward to her reaction. In spite of what she thought, he understood her a little too well. Nancy was going to hate what he had to say to her. No matter how gentle he tried to be, the truth was going to hurt. He only hoped it wouldn't kill their relationship.

> Waiting, the quiet café the ghosts
> of others who left me here
> alone, wondering.
> Shadows march across the walls
> in silent grief procession.

> What can I do to prove to you I am serious? SSS, I don't understand. What happened? Name another time, another place. Take your time. I'll wait for you. TDH.

Soozie's eyes blurred as she stared at the monitor. TDH was full of poems and gentle words again. She sniffed back her tears and quickly looked around the computer center. Every cubby was occupied with the usual late-afternoon crowd. But to her relief, everyone's eyes were glued to their own screen. No one had seen her almost break down.

Soozie sat up straighter, then printed out TDH's message, as she had every single one, good or bad. She wasn't sure how to answer him now. She decided to wait until the next day. Then she noticed another message in her mailbox. She retrieved it. Her eyes widened as she read.

> SSS, oooooh. I know a secret about you. You *bribed* some guy to take you to your high school prom. . . .

"What?" Soozie blurted, then slammed her hand over her mouth. How in the world . . . no one, but no one, knew about that. She had campaigned to get herself nominated for prom queen, but her date fell through the night before. She had been desperate and was proud of how she had managed to salvage the situation. But no one in the world knew about it. Except the guy, who was her second cousin, who went to the University of Omaha now. High school was so long ago, Soozie had practically forgotten all about that prom disaster. Soozie bent closer to the screen and read on.

> If you don't meet me by the lake, I just might post this tasty bit of news on the Net. You'll never hear the end of it. And there's more where that came from. . . . TDH

Soozie read the message again. I don't believe this! Suddenly she realized exactly where TDH had gotten the scoop on her prom problems—her diary. Somehow he had gotten hold of her diary.

Soozie moistened her lips and forced herself to call up the next message.

SSS—So *you're* giving *me* the silent treat-
ment this time around, just like I gave you last
night on the phone. It won't work, you know. I'm
not the kind of guy who reacts well to rejection.

> Linked in crime, linked in hate
> Love turned cruel is love too late
> Kisses in the twisted dark
> Death can play the silent part
> TDH

Soozie broke out in a cold sweat. Wow, this
guy was seriously schizo or something. One minute he was kind, the next horrible. Worse yet, he
had tracked her down to the sorority house *and*
had gotten his hands on her diary. She had bared
her heart and soul and deepest, darkest secrets
in there. She'd die if he posted entries about her
on the Usenet. What if he didn't stop at crank
calls and petty theft?

Soozie suddenly felt dizzy. What if he attacked
her or some other Kappa? What did he mean
about death?

"Hey, Soozie, what's new?" Nick said, coming
up behind her.

His voice made her jump.

She whirled around in her chair and gasped.
"Will you stop spying on me?"

Nick lifted his hands in protest. "Whoa. You're
touchy these days. I'm not spying. I'm being
friendly. Part of my job, you know." His pleasant
face shifted into a scowl. "I don't get it. You

seem like a nice person, and then you turn on people. . . ." His voice trailed off.

Soozie noticed he was squinting over her shoulder at the screen. She quickly shut off the machine. "Mind your own business," she commanded, reaching for her purse and snatching the copies of TDH's messages out of the printer.

"Fine! A real Jekyll and Hyde," he muttered.

Soozie got up from her chair and brushed past him. She didn't need the whole world looking over her shoulder at the nasty messages some sicko had been transmitting to her.

She burst out of the dark basement of Graves Hall into the slanting late-afternoon sun. She marched down the Walk a few more steps, then stopped in her tracks. Jekyll and Hyde.

Soozie thought back to the famous story of the scientist who took some potion and one minute was sweet as pie and the next became a homicidal monster. She looked back over her shoulder at Graves Hall.

What an insult! She was *not* like that. Soozie felt a stab of conscience. Actually, she had just accused him of spying. But generally she thought she had been pretty nice to him, considering he was just a guy who worked there. Okay, a *cute* guy. And he had always been helpful and sweet to her.

Sorry, Nick, she apologized inwardly. But thanks, too. He had given her the perfect description of her "nightmare" man.

The problem was, TDH wasn't just turning into *her* nightmare. He had become Kappa's nightmare, too, Soozie thought as she headed toward the sorority house. Soozie sighed. She had a distinctly uneasy feeling that she shouldn't keep her suspicions about TDH to herself. But the very thought of admitting to the other girls that she had something to do with those calls made her sick.

Still, Soozie sensed that real trouble could be brewing. TDH had figured out she was a Kappa. He had figured out she was blond. But so were Holly and half a dozen other sisters who lived in the house.

Every one of them could be in jeopardy. Soozie wasn't a fan of Holly, but that didn't mean she wanted some sicko to attack her.

Soozie had to confide her fears to someone. She was in over her head and definitely needed help. She needed to talk to someone in the sorority. She didn't want campus authorities involved unless things got really out of hand. There had been one too many scandals involving Greek Row this year, and Soozie didn't want her sorority singled out by the administration as one of the "problem" houses.

But who in Kappa could she trust?

Soozie blew out her breath, and after another hurried glance over her shoulder, ducked in the side door.

As she headed for her room, inspiration struck. There was somebody. She wasn't a friend, exactly, but Soozie sensed she would never turn down a sister in trouble, no matter what bad blood lay between them.

CHAPTER 7

No wonder you didn't want to have breakfast at the Kappa house today," Bess remarked to Holly. After a second night of nuisance calls, Holly had called Bess early Thursday to meet in the Jamison Hall cafeteria. Holly needed feedback on the situation. They had run into Eileen O'Connor and Casey in the food line.

Holly poked at her oatmeal, but she felt too tired to eat. "Really," she said now. "The whole thing has everyone in the house on edge."

"I know the feeling," Casey sympathized. "When that stalker was trailing me, everything and everyone made me nervous. That kind of weirdo could be anyone you know—or a complete stranger. That's the frightening part."

"Well," Bess said with determined cheer, "at least you've made a plan. The phone company will give you suggestions."

Holly made a face. "I know. But I hate going

outside the sorority to solve this." Holly hesitated. "And then there's more."

"More than the calls?" Casey looked worried.

"Have you been on-line lately?" she asked Eileen.

Eileen shook her head. Holly went on. "Some really nasty messages about Kappas have been posted. By someone who has the *inside* scoop on people who live at the house. Listen to this." Holly pulled some papers out of her bag. "I printed this stuff out last night before I went to bed." Holly read out loud.

" 'Someone's got it in for the Kappas. I wonder who's been snooping around the dear old house lately and getting the scoop. Our informant tells us that one sister's in the kitchen baking up a storm and getting every one as fat as she is.' "

"That's about Leila, and it's so mean!" Casey cried. "I hope she didn't see that."

"Oh, it gets better," Holly said with a tight laugh. "This might be referring to yours truly: 'A certain Kappa bleached her eyebrows last night to match her golden hair. Now she has to bleach her hair to match her eyebrows because they turned out green.' "

Bess cracked up. "That's you. But who would post that on the Net?"

"The same person who posted this bit about Darcy's having two dates on the same night and going out with both, one after the other. And this last one is definitely about Janie." Holly read again: " 'Sometimes I think she might be a great performance artist one day, because behind that shy exterior lurks a tough, shrewd woman. I'm sure of it. . . .' "

"Not too damning," Casey said, musing. "But definitely embarrassing to find personal stuff about yourself posted for everyone to see."

Bess looked thoughtful. "Maybe it's the Zetas again. Whenever Kappa's being hassled, Zeta is usually behind it."

"No," Eileen said in contradiction. "Emmet would have told me. He tells me everything, and he definitely would have spilled the beans about this."

"Maybe not," Bess said. "Emmet's a prankster himself, or do I have to remind you?"

Holly cleared her throat and caught Casey's eye. "Bess," she reminded gently, "there just haven't been any Zeta pranks lately. Ever since Paul died."

Her words hung in the air a second. Then Bess said, "What's that got to do with it? A Zeta is a Zeta. I still think they might be the culprits." Her smile was bright, but Holly heard the tension in Bess's voice.

"Bess," Casey said, "the point is that everyone's still upset about Paul."

"Only natural," Bess said, gulping down her coffee. "But guys will be guys. Especially *frat* guys."

Holly sighed. "Bess, I don't know about that . . ." she started to say, but before she could get out any more, Soozie walked up to the table.

"Oh, Bess," she said, glancing around the little group. "I went to your room, but Leslie told me you had already left for breakfast. She should have told me with whom." Soozie looked ready to bolt.

"You were looking for *me?*" Bess sounded amazed.

After a moment Soozie nodded. "I need to talk to you."

"I think," Holly said, beginning to push back her chair, "that she wants the rest of us to get lost."

"No," Soozie said quickly. "This actually involves all of you. You guys will never believe what happened." Soozie pulled up a chair and began to tell them all about TDH.

"The guy you met on-line really turned out to be a jerk," Holly said, smiling in spite of herself when Soozie had finished her story. "Forgive me for not feeling completely sympathetic."

"I deserve it," Soozie admitted with difficulty. "But look, I'm really freaked, and not just for me."

"I believe it," Bess assured her.

"Look, Sooze, I'd feel pretty awkward in your shoes right now. But, hey, we're all allowed to change our minds. . . ."

"Or make mistakes," Soozie said, sounding miserable. "Of course mine happens to be a big one. . . ."

"It's fitting," Casey teased gently. "So what now?"

"You mean you guys aren't upset with me?" Soozie said, amazed.

"Yeah. We're upset." Holly laughed and pointed to her eyes. "Last night's calls were so bad that I used up a year's supply of concealer to hide the damage. But we're Kappas, so let's see if we can pull together to solve the situation."

"How?" Soozie asked.

"I wish I could help," Eileen said, "but I've got to meet Montana now."

"And we have to go to class," Casey reminded Bess.

"That's true," Bess said, gathering up her books. "But I think I can get you some major-league help. I know exactly whom you need to talk to."

"Nancy?" Jake called, knocking at the door of her room in Thayer Hall.

At the sound of Jake's voice, Nancy drew a quick breath and checked her reflection in the mirror.

"Get a grip, girl," she told herself, then hurried to the door and threw it open. "Jake," she greeted him and a second later was in his arms. She lifted her face to his for a kiss. So much love shone in his eyes that it took her breath away.

He bent down and brushed her lips lightly. She leaned against him, but gently, firmly, he put her at arm's length. Jake had an all-business look that took the life right out of her.

"Nancy," he said a bit huskily, walking in the

room and closing the door behind him. "Let's not get distracted."

Nancy folded her arms across her chest and met his gaze directly. "Right," she said, and sat on the edge of her bed.

Jake didn't sit beside her. He pulled up her desk chair and sat down facing her. He gave a nervous smile, then began. "Let's talk . . . first."

"Then?" Nancy couldn't help but tease him. Now that they were going to talk things out, she was sure somehow they'd bridge whatever gap had opened between them.

Jake didn't flirt back. "Look, I've thought a lot about why we're out of sync. Ever since we came back from River Heights that weekend . . ."

"River Heights," she repeated, her mood darkening. "Not that again."

"Not what, Nancy? Sometimes I think you're just determined not to hear me out on this one."

"Jake," she said, jumping up and walking to the window. "It's not that I didn't want to hear you. I've been listening all along—to *your* take on the whole thing. But maybe the problem between us has nothing to do with that weekend."

"But it does," Jake insisted. "You've accused me of not knowing what was going on back there on your home turf. But it was obvious. You're having trouble with Avery's dating your father, and for some reason you're taking it out on me."

"That's not true," Nancy said, contradicting him. "Avery and my dad are one issue. What's going on with us is another, Jake."

"Is it?" Jake asked. "I don't think so. You can't face your real feelings—whatever they are—about what's going on in River Heights. And that scares me. It makes me think you can't face your real feelings about us. I don't really know what you feel about me anymore!" Jake exclaimed, sounding hurt.

"How can you say that?" Nancy felt as if he had punched her in the stomach. What about the way he had walked in the room just now and touched her, and the way she couldn't keep her hands off him? "I think it's pretty obvious we've got some pretty strong feelings for each other, Jake."

Nancy stood across the room from him, her hands folded across her chest. Jake leaned back in his chair, avoiding her eyes.

Jake broke the silence first. "In spite of those feelings, lately all we do is fight," he said sadly.

"I don't want to," Nancy said, reaching out for him. Jake stood and crossed the room to take Nancy's hand. "But sometimes, Jake Collins, you just make me so mad," she said softly.

"I've noticed." He dropped her hand and looked her in the eye. "And I just don't know why."

"That's the problem!" Nancy said, hoping he would hear her through. "But here's an example of what really sets me off. Back when I insisted on following my own leads on that *Wilder Times* story about Cal Evanson, you took Gail Gardeski's side."

"Nan, what are you dredging that up for?"
Jake said hotly. "I wasn't taking sides. I was just
trying to protect Gail's right to protect her
source."

"That's just part of it. You admitted you felt I
wasn't experienced enough and that it wasn't fair
for a freshman to snare a lead story like that,"
Nancy said in challenge. "But speaking of not
dealing with feelings, I think you were threatened
by my getting the scoop. Until then, I believed
we were supposed to be partners."

"Wrong. You think I'm supposed to be your
yes-man," Jake countered hotly. "Well, I can't
be. And I won't. I tell things like I see them."

"Right, and of course the way *you* see them
is always right, Jake, like the way you 'saw' my
relationship with my dad and Avery. Or the way
you 'saw' me with Terry the other night." Nancy
wished she'd kept her mouth shut.

Jake's mouth fell open. "What do you want
from me?" he cried finally. "I said I believed you
about Terry. I don't love the guy. I don't love
the fact he's supposed to be your *friend*, but I
said I trust you."

Before Nancy could even begin to answer that,
the phone rang.

"Great!" Jake grumbled, throwing his hands in
the air and sitting heavily at the foot of Nancy's
bed.

"Who can that be?" Nancy said, annoyed, and
snatched up the receiver. "Hello?" she barked.

"Nancy?" Bess sounded confused. "Bad timing?"

Nancy swept her hair off her face. She forced herself to sound calm. "Sort of. But we can talk a little, Bess. What's up?" She kept her eyes averted from Jake as she listened to Bess and tried to pull herself together.

"There's a big problem at Kappa. Soozie and Holly need to talk to you."

"Me?" Nancy heaved a sigh. "Look, I don't want to get involved in some sort of Kappa intrigue."

"It's not intrigue, Nancy. At least I don't think so," Bess said. "But they really need your help. Listen to this. . . ."

As Bess relayed the story about the caller and Soozie's disastrous on-line relationship with TDH, Nancy's interest grew. "This sounds pretty serious," she said thoughtfully. She glanced over her shoulder at Jake, and suddenly she was inspired.

He was pacing in front of her door, checking his watch. She knew he had a heavy schedule that day, but Bess's call gave her an idea. Jake was good at figuring things out. At least things that had nothing to do with her, she reminded herself. Ferreting out an on-line sicko might be right up Jake's alley. It would sure give them a chance to investigate a problem together, and there might even be a story in it for the paper. And working together might be a way to work out their relationship.

"Look, where are Holly and Soozie?" Nancy asked Bess. "Tell them to wait, and I'll pick them up and we can head off to Kappa to see what's up." Nancy got the information from Bess, hung up, then turned to Jake.

"Jake, I'm sorry I got a little worked up back there," she said.

Jake acted a little sheepish. "Me, too. I guess we both have some stuff bottled up."

"We'll get back to this later, but now there's a heavy-duty problem brewing at Kappa, and Bess asked me to help out two of her sisters."

"Now?" He looked less than thrilled.

Nancy made herself smile. "Hey, Jake, I know the timing's crummy, but maybe we need a time-out. Why don't you come with me and help me figure out what's in the works? It has to do with the Usenet and some creepo scaring Soozie Beckerman."

Jake's lips narrowed. "She probably deserves it."

"Jake?" Nancy said, surprised.

Jake looked guilty. "Okay, I'll come along for the ride, but I really would rather just spend the time with you working things out, Nancy."

"For now, let's settle for the spending time together part," Nancy said, taking his hand. Jake instantly curled his fingers around hers.

His touch reassured Nancy. She relaxed a little. He did still want them to solve their problems. A good sign!

*　　*　　*

Ginny Yuen sat in the lounge of suite 301, laughing at her roommate Liz Bader's tale of her latest Architecture 101 assignment.

"You're too much, Liz. Why did you volunteer to design a whole neighborhood?" Ginny asked.

"She's a glutton for punishment," Reva Ross remarked.

"Wrong," Liz corrected in her throaty voice. "I'm determined to make Professor Krass notice me. I want to stand out. I want an A."

"And his being an absolute hunk has nothing to do with this?" Ginny tossed a cushion at her roommate.

"Who's a hunk?" Eileen asked, sauntering into the lounge. Montana was right behind her.

"Liz's professor," Ginny replied, but eyed Montana warily. She didn't *want* to be jealous of her, but Montana had made no secret of her crush on Ray.

"Look, Eileen, let's get back to the point," Montana said. She and Eileen crossed the small common area and parked themselves at a table in the corner. "I spoke to Ray the other day, and he's agreed to a radio interview tomorrow."

At the sound of Ray's name, Ginny looked up quickly. Montana was glowing. Ginny tried to focus her attention back on Liz and Reva's conversation, but she couldn't help eavesdropping. How did Montana snare Ray for an interview? He hated interviews.

"I think you should get Emmet's brother,

Jason, to listen to the show and invite Radical Moves to perform at Club Z," Montana urged.

Eileen pursed her lips. "The point is, Montana, that I don't have a thing to do with what acts Jason Lehman books for the club. I'm dating Emmet, not his brother. I'm not that tight with Jason. Besides," Eileen said, "Radical Moves has to make its own decisions about the club. If they want a club date, let them set it up."

"That's what I told them. I also told Ray how unbelievably terrific he is."

Eileen laughed softly. "I'm sure you did."

Ginny frowned.

Montana laughed outright. "Well, that, too." She dropped her voice, and Ginny couldn't hear her for a second. Then Montana said in a more normal tone, "Would you believe the whole lot of them don't think they're ready yet? I mean, gimme a break. These guys are so terrific. They're just scared, that's what I think."

"Well, it's their call, Montana, not yours and not mine and not even Jason's. They have to do what feels right to them," Eileen pointed out.

Ginny agreed, but she wished Montana didn't feel so invested in Ray. Ginny wondered if Montana cared at all about Ray's music. To Ray, music was the whole world. Singing and playing guitar were his life.

Montana probably just had a crush on him because of his looks. Ray did have star quality.

But the Ray Ginny knew was more than a star.

He was a deep-feeling, sensitive guy who had touched her heart as no one else had.

"Hey, Ginny, anyone home in there?" Liz asked.

Ginny blushed and laughed. "Just out to lunch," she joked. But inside, her thoughts were spinning. If Montana's interest in Ray made her jealous, maybe she should look to the state of her own heart. Maybe Ginny should never have left Ray in the first place.

"What I don't understand," Holly remarked from the backseat of Nancy's Mustang, "is how this on-line creep figured out that Soozie's a Kappa. Did you tell him?" she asked Soozie.

"Tell him?" Soozie said nervously. "My name? No. And I never mentioned Kappa House. I'm sure of it."

"Maybe something else you said gave him a hint," Nancy suggested as she pulled the car into the circular drive in front of the sorority house. "There's also a chance the nuisance calls have nothing to do with you, Soozie, or that guy."

"I'm sure they do," Soozie said. "He mentioned the phone in his last message to me. That's too much of a coincidence."

"Well, he sure sounds like a creep, right, Jake?" Nancy asked, glancing across the seat.

"Uh—yeah, a real loser," Jake answered, unable to conceal his boredom.

"I think this might make an interesting story for the paper," Holly suggested to him.

"It might." He flashed a tentative smile at Nancy. "But we'd have to go to Gail with it first, and she'd assign a reporter. Probably someone with more experience with the Usenet."

'Haven't you ever gone on-line?" Nancy asked Jake, trying to keep him involved in the conversation.

"Not much. It gets to be habit-forming. All I've done is surf the Net a few times to research articles and check out references for papers."

Jake's tone was curt, and as they piled out of the car and into the sorority house, Nancy decided it was going to be a long morning.

"I have copies of some of TDH's messages, poetry and all," Soozie said, tossing her coat and bag on one of the two long sofas flanking the fireplace.

"It might be good to see them," Nancy said, then added tactfully, "if you don't mind sharing them."

Soozie flashed her a grateful look. "I asked you for help. The least I can do is help you. But can you kind of not show them around?" she asked Nancy, but caught Holly's eye.

'Don't worry, I won't broadcast your love notes, Soozie," Holly promised with a laugh. "Though I'd be tempted."

Soozie went up to her room, while Holly fixed some herbal tea. Nancy walked around the large common area and noticed there was a house phone just outside in the foyer. Hadn't Holly mentioned a phone at the top of the stairs?

When she ambled back to the couch, Jake had buried himself in the newspaper. Nancy frowned at him, wishing he could at least pretend to be helpful. With a loud sigh, she sat down and stared at his paper, wishing she could bore holes in it with her eyes.

What was the point? Jake was not in the mood to investigate anything, let alone a rash of strange phone calls at Kappa House.

A stack of poetry books on the coffee table caught her eye. Who was into poetry at Kappa? Maybe Soozie had started reading poetry after TDH sent her some on-line. Nancy picked up the top book.

"Sylvia Plath," she said, reading the author's name aloud. She flipped through the pages. She remembered reading something by Sylvia Plath in high school. "Hey, Jake, what do you know about Sylvia Plath's poetry?" she asked, skimming one of the pages. The poem was extraordinary, strong, but gloomy for Nancy's taste.

"I've read her," Jake said, tossing aside the paper. He peered over Nancy's shoulder and read a few lines. "Not my thing, really."

"Not mine either," Nancy said, putting the book down as Darcy walked in.

Nancy made room for her on the couch. "Soozie and Holly asked me to come over to talk about the phone calls the house has been getting."

"A real drag," Darcy said. "No one's sleeping."

Holly walked in with the herbal tea and smiled at Darcy. "Did you sleep last night?"

"Not a wink. I answered the phone twice myself."

"And no one was on the other end?" Nancy asked.

"Not a soul. Freaky."

"Do any of you have any idea what might be going on?" Nancy asked, sipping some tea.

"Not a clue," Darcy remarked.

"Um, Nancy?" Jake spoke up suddenly. When Nancy wasn't looking, he had grabbed his jacket and was standing by the door. "Look, I've got a meeting with one of my professors. Gotta fly."

Nancy knew perfectly well that Jake just wanted out of there. She felt disappointed and a little hurt.

"See you later," he called back in her general direction.

"Right." Nancy tried to sound cheerful. But she wondered what they'd say to each other next time they were alone. Whenever that might be.

As Jake headed through the common room door, Janie walked in past him. Nancy looked up and smiled at her.

"Hi, Nancy," Janie said. "What brings you here?"

"Those crazy phone calls that are keeping everyone up in the house," Nancy said. "You're a senior. Do you ever remember anything like this happening at Kappa before?"

Janie frowned, grabbing a stack of books off

the coffee table. "No, not really. I mean people are always playing tricks in sororities."

"That's what Bess said," Holly commented. "She thought Zeta might be involved. But we're thinking it might have something to do with Soozie."

Janie's eyebrows arched up. "Like what?"

"I'm not sure," Nancy said. "But she's got some personal problems that might tie in with the calls."

"Sorry to hear that." Janie checked her watch.

"You *are?*" Holly laughed. "That's a turnaround."

"Like I told you before, why hold grudges?"

"Well, someone's holding a big one," Nancy commented grimly. "And they're pestering not just Soozie, but all the Kappas."

CHAPTER 8

"Let's take a break," Brian suggested to Bess and Casey Thursday afternoon. "For some reason," he said, eyeballing Bess, "this improv is a lost cause."

"*I'm* a lost cause." Bess tried to look contrite from where she was sitting on the floor of a rehearsal room. "I just can't focus."

Casey playfully slapped Bess with her sweatshirt before pulling it over her head. "Bess, you *have* been a million miles away all day."

"Not quite a million miles," Bess quipped, pulling a bottle of water out of her backpack. "More like a few hundred yards. As far as Kappa house."

"You're still thinking about that mess?" Casey seemed surprised.

Bess chuckled. "The more I think about it, the more I'm sure the Zetas are behind the whole thing. You know what a bunch of jokers those guys are. I wouldn't be surprised if one of them turned out to be Soozie's on-line sicko boyfriend."

"Yeah," Brian said skeptically. "What's going on at Kappa is sicker than even Zeta's usual style."

"I'm sure it's not really that big a deal. Soozie just got unnerved," Bess insisted, then added after a moment, "I think it's pretty hilarious. The whole house talks about nothing else. I should call Zeta and give them something with real shock value."

"Like what?" Casey asked.

"Like call and pretend it's Paul's ghost. Booooooooo!" Bess wriggled her fingers at Casey and Brian. The whole idea struck Bess as so funny that she doubled over laughing.

Casey and Paul looked at Bess in horror.

Bess straightened up and stared at them. "What's with you two?"

"Bess," Brian said very quietly, "the question is, what's with you?"

She returned his frown. *"Now* what did I do?"

"How can you joke about Paul like that?" Casey asked, shocked.

Bess averted her eyes from Casey's and fiddled with the lace of her sneaker. "Because if I don't start joking about Paul, I'm going to cry. It's one or the other." Her voice grew lower with every word. "If I begin to cry, I can't stop. I can't eat. I can't sleep. I just lie in my room curled in a ball and sob. That's not very healthy." Finally, she said in a whisper, "I can't stand it anymore. If I let myself think about Paul, it hurts so much I can barely breathe. It's physical." She brought her hand to her chest. "But if I try to laugh and brush things off, I get through. Minute by minute. Day by day."

Even now Bess could barely force back the sob that was about to burst out of her.

Brian got up and crossed over to where Bess was sitting. He pulled her to her feet and drew her to him and cradled her in a big hug. In his arms, Bess felt almost safe and whole again. "Bri," she murmured into his flannel shirt. "You're such a good friend."

"You have a lot of very good friends here," Casey said, joining them. For a moment, they all hugged. Then Bess pulled away and rubbed her sleeve across her face.

Casey put one arm around Bess's shoulder, and said softly, "Look, let's stop rehearsing now and do something together. We could head into town and shop, or—"

"No," Bess said. "I'm not in the mood to shop, Casey. Maybe I'll check in with Vicky, my counselor. I do need to talk to someone."

"I'll walk you over to her office," Brian offered. "Maybe she'll see you now."

"No. I'll go alone. I'm really okay."

"But you'll talk to her today?" Casey asked.

"I'll try to," Bess promised. And she would call. But she was beginning to wonder if her counselor was the person she really needed to talk to.

Soozie wasn't supposed to meet Nancy at the computer lab for at least forty-five minutes. But she bounded down the steps of Graves Hall into the basement early. She was really grateful that Bess's friend had agreed to help her, but she was also wary. She hadn't told anyone about her diary and that horrid excerpt TDH had taunted her with. Right after reading it, she had raced back to her room: Sure enough, her diary was gone. How he had found out where she lived was a mystery. Soozie pushed back a knot of fear. She had to put a stop to this before it went too far. Her whole reputation—if not something more—was on the line here.

Nancy's crowd, including Holly, were not among Soozie's biggest fans. Soozie hated giving them ammunition against her. When she showed Nancy the copies of her E-mail, she had shown her only the ones that didn't mention the diary or that prom disaster.

Now maybe, with a little luck, she could get out of it on her own before Nancy turned up. She checked her makeup in the glass window of the door. After tucking a stray strand of hair behind her ear, Soozie moistened her lips and walked into the lab.

It took only a moment to spot the dark-haired guy leaning over someone's terminal. Sensing someone's gaze on him, Nick O'Donnell looked up. His eyebrows arched at the sight of her.

Soozie put on her prettiest smile and waved three fingers at him. It worked like a charm, and Soozie felt a familiar thrill of power as he crossed the room toward her. This guy sure had a crush on her.

"So, what's new?" he asked pleasantly, as if he hadn't called her Jekyll and Hyde the other day. Soozie decided to forget the insult for now.

"I have a problem, and I thought you were just the man to help me solve it."

"Oh?" Nick was curious.

Soozie leaned back against the wall and lowered her voice to an intimate whisper. "It's sort of private."

Nick bent down to hear her better. He wore a sultry aftershave that Soozie fond intoxicating in spite of herself.

"Is there a way to trace E-mail?" she asked, batting her eyes at him.

Nick straightened up and eyed her cautiously. "Why?"

"Oh, I met someone on-line, and I want to know who he is before I take the chance of meeting with him."

"No," Nick said with a firm shake of his head. "That's not fair. Besides, tracing E-mail isn't very honest. Anyway, the point of on-line dating is that *everyone* is in the dark."

Soozie nodded. "I know that. But can't you

break the rules just once? Especially when some-one's acting like a real psycho?"

"Psycho!" Nick reacted loudly.

"Sshhhh!" Soozie tried to silence him. She was suddenly afraid that whoever TDH was, he could be lurking anywhere—in the computer room even, listening to them.

"What psycho?" Nick acted totally confused. "What are you talking about?"

Soozie swallowed hard. She had come to Nick for help. How could he help if he didn't know what was going on? She plucked out one of the printouts from her bag and handed it to him. "I met this guy on-line. At first I really liked him, but then he flipped out or something. Check out these messages and you'll see what I mean."

Nick sat down in the stairwell and quickly began to read. As Soozie watched, his cheeks turned red. He jumped up and shoved the paper back in her hand. He searched Soozie's eyes a moment, then without a word turned and raced up the stairs.

"What was that about?" Soozie wondered out loud.

Nancy headed straight for Graves Hall after her English lit class. She had promised to meet Soozie to check out her E-mail and to see if she could begin making sense out of TDH's crazy messages.

Not that she was in the mood to help Soozie

or anyone solve her problems just now. She had enough of her own, with Jake topping the list.

As Nancy crossed the Walk, she replayed every word of her conversation with Jake that morning. What had gone wrong? Their meeting had only made things go from bad to worse.

He still had no idea where she was coming from. He wouldn't listen to her. He had his own stubborn view of the situation and nothing she said or did would change that. She had already told him she'd deal with Avery and her dad—in her own way.

She hadn't yet, but she would, Nancy told herself. And Jake for some reason insisted on taking Avery's *and* her dad's side. At least she had tried to communicate with Jake. But as far as she could tell, he wasn't trying at all. He had taken a position and was sticking to it like Krazy Glue.

When Nancy arrived at the lab, she noticed that there was no one staffing the help desk at the front of the room. Too bad. She knew her way around the Wilder Usenet, had gone on-line now and then just for the fun of it, and out of curiosity, had E-mailed friends from River Heights who had gone to college on the West Coast. But Nancy wasn't a computer expert and had hoped the operations manager would be around in case she had questions.

As usual, most of the terminals in the lab were occupied. She looked around and spotted Soozie's blond head at the far end of one of the banks of computers.

Nancy made her way toward Soozie. "Any more messages?" she asked, wondering why the Kappa seemed twice as frazzled as she had that morning.

Soozie looked up and relief washed over her face. "Am I glad to see you!"

"Nice to know I'm wanted," Nancy said evenly. "What's up?" She sat down next to Soozie.

Soozie frowned. "Weird stuff. That's all."

"More creepy messages?" Nancy asked.

"That, too." Soozie sat back and folded her hands in her lap. Nancy could tell she was debating whether to tell her something. "I don't know. Maybe it's nothing. Why don't you check out this latest batch of messages first?" Soozie suggested, getting up and motioning for Nancy to take the seat in front of the screen.

Nancy sensed Soozie was holding something back. She clicked the mouse and retrieved the last of the E-mail messages Soozie had saved. She pondered the screen a moment. "Poetry again?" she murmured, then remembered what she wanted to ask Soozie. "Do you read poetry?"

"My poetry reading's pretty much limited to what TDH writes on-screen," she said, a little embarrassed. "I told him I'd start, but I haven't yet. I had the best intentions, but then these messages got weird."

"This doesn't seem to be a weird one," Nancy said as she read the message.

SSS—I don't know what's scared you off. I could put this in my own words, but that poet I told you about says it better.

> What is there to fear but love
> That devours fear the way the sun
> Devours the night sky
> Until dark breaks open its shell and day
>   flies
> Out, a startled white bird

Please meet me. Tell me what's wrong in person. TDH

"That's beautiful," Nancy said, the poetry touching her. The words reminded her of Jake and how she really felt about him, no matter how bad things were now. But as she reread them, they reminded her of something else. But what?

"Yeah," Stephanie remarked, "but wait till you see the next one." She shuddered as Nancy checked out the next message. Then the next and the next. The messages almost alternated from cruel and creepy to soft, sweet, and romantic.

"Should I print these, too?" Soozie asked, peeking over Nancy's shoulder at the monitor.

"Might as well," Nancy said, perplexed and more than a little worried. She leaned back in the chair and thought aloud. "TDH is one complicated guy."

"Hard to figure, isn't it? One minute, all sugar

and spice; the next, he comes on like something from a horror movie." Soozie's laugh sounded forced.

Nancy fingered the printed copies of TDH's messages The nasty ones almost read as if they were replying to the nice ones, poetry and all— as if two different people were having some kind of argument. Were they dealing with someone who had multiple personalities? "Like Jekyll and Hyde," Nancy remarked aloud to Soozie.

Soozie's blue eyes widened. "Right, that's just what Nick said."

"Nick?" Nancy straightened up. "Who's Nick?"

To Nancy's surprise, Soozie blushed.

"Soozie, if you want me to help you, you've got to tell me *everything* that's going on here. Who's Nick?"

"It's not what you think," Soozie informed her quickly. "It's just Nick O'Donnell. He said *I* was like Jekyll and Hyde."

"You?" Nancy could think of lots of unflattering ways to describe Soozie Beckerman. Cool. Power hungry. Cutthroat competitive at times. Self-centered and vain. But Jekyll and Hyde didn't quite fit.

"Can you believe he said that about me?" Soozie asked, annoyed. "Just because I told him to mind his own business when he walked up behind me the other day and started reading one of TDH's messages on my screen."

"So *he* saw one of the messages?" Nancy grew thoughtful. "What was he doing here?"

"Oh," Soozie told her, "he's the lab's systems administrator. He helped me navigate my way around the Usenet the first time I came here. He showed me how to sign on and find my way into the chat room."

"Ah!" Nancy exclaimed. Then something occurred to her. "But that means he's probably some kind of computer whiz."

"Tell me about. He's a regular nerd. Though you couldn't tell by looking at the guy. He's a real hunk. Tall, dark . . ."

"And handsome." Nancy supplied the missing word. "TDH."

"Nick?" Soozie gasped. Nancy watched Soozie's expression go from shock, to disbelief, to wonder, to fear. "Oh, Nancy," she cried, and sat down heavily on her chair. "I hope you're wrong."

"Why? Do you like him?" Nancy pried gently.

"No," Soozie answered a little too quickly. "I mean, I don't think so. But just now, before you came in, I . . . now you're going to think I'm a total creep."

Nancy tried to keep her smile neutral.

"I thought I could save us both trouble if I tried to figure out who TDH was myself. So I came here early for our appointment. I thought Nick might help me out." Soozie went on to describe Nick's reaction to seeing the printed messages.

As Nancy listened, her suspicions strengthened. "That was pretty weird for him to rush off like that."

"I know," Soozie said dismally. "He could be TDH, now that I think of it. He did know my handle. He was there when I picked it. I didn't realize I was such a bad judge of people."

"I didn't say it was him for sure. There's no way of knowing just yet. But he did help you sign on. And that would explain his knowing you were a Kappa."

"True," Soozie said, fingering the little gold sorority pin on her shirt. "But I told TDH enough on-line about myself so that someone who had never seen me could figure that out. Yet Nick did seem concerned when I told him that I was never going on-line again."

"His concern might be genuine," Nancy said, not wanting to jump to any conclusions about Nick. "Maybe that's why he was so upset today when you showed him the messages. It's possible that you're not the only person being hassled, and since he's in charge here, he knows about something bigger going on."

"Could be," Soozie agreed. "One more thing. All this poetry TDH has sent, the good stuff and the bad, it's from the confessional poets. He told me that. Do you know who they are?"

Nancy tried to place them. "It rings a bell. I'll check it out, but right now, I think we've got to flush this guy out. I think you should post a message agreeing to meet him after all."

"No way!" Soozie cried, horrified.

Nancy made a calming gesture. "Insist it be in a public place. Tonight. Then let me know where. I'm going to be there with Holly."

"Holly?" Soozie scowled. "Why her?"

"Because she's vice-president of Kappa, and TDH or whoever is making these phone calls is hassling the whole house," Nancy pointed out.

"Right," Soozie conceded. "I've already made a fool of myself with this whole on-line mess. She might as well gloat some more while I play the complete idiot and meet this weirdo."

Nancy heard the fear lurking beneath Soozie's hard-edged sarcasm. "You're not being an idiot for doing this. Holly and I aren't coming along to laugh at you. We're there to be sure nothing happens."

"Right," Soozie said skeptically.

CHAPTER 9

What if he notices us?" Holly said to Nancy that night in Anthony's, the off-campus club where Soozie agreed to meet TDH. The place was jammed. Soozie sat at the next table nervously jabbing a straw at the ice in her soda, her eyes darting around the room as she tried to pick out TDH.

"Good chance that TDH—whoever he is— doesn't even know us, or suspect we know Soozie," Nancy hurried to assure Holly. "But how are we supposed to eavesdrop on them over all this noise?"

"Wouldn't you know it's a heavy-metal band. Why couldn't this be one of Anthony's unplugged nights!" Holly put her hands over her ears.

Nancy laughed as she ordered their sodas. "Pretty inconvenient. When I said set up a date in a public place, I didn't mean somewhere this loud and crowded."

Holly gestured toward Soozie's table, "What happened to the famous Beckerman cool?"

Nancy followed Holly's gaze. Soozie was tearing her napkin to shreds.

Holly suddenly clutched Nancy's arm. "Check out that guy."

Nancy casually scanned the club. A tall, dark-haired guy was approaching Soozie's table. "TDH?" she murmured. He was definitely handsome. He wore a gray Wilder sweatshirt with red lettering. He looked nervous. Nancy shifted her glance to Soozie. Soozie was staring at the guy, confused. "I think she knows him," Nancy told Holly. Soozie cast a quick panicky glance at Nancy.

"Me, too. But how?" Holly said.

Nancy motioned for Holly to be quiet. She wanted to hear what Soozie had to say.

"Hi, Nick." Soozie's mouth was so dry she could barely say his name. Was TDH really Nick after all? Soozie shot a panicked glance at Nancy. "What are you doing here?" She put her hand up to stop him from sitting down. "Sorry, this seat is taken. I'm waiting for someone."

Nick sat down. "I know," he said, glancing back over his shoulder.

"How—how do you know I'm meeting someone here?" Soozie didn't want to believe this was happening.

"Because I'm TDH," he admitted.

Soozie almost screamed. Then she remembered nothing would happen to her here. Not in the crowded club. Not so long as Holly and Nancy were a couple of seats away. Keeping her eyes fixed on Nick's, she slowly pushed her chair back from the table.

"Stop, Soozie," he begged, reaching for her hand.

Soozie pulled away but continued to listen.

"Hear me out. I'm TDH, but I'm no weirdo."

Soozie stared at him. "Why did you run today when I showed you that printout?"

"Because I freaked out. I E-mailed you poems, not threats."

"I'm supposed to believe this?" Soozie scoffed.

"It's true," Nick declared. "I don't know who's been messing with the system, but somehow someone else knows our handles and is playing games."

"Games? It seems to me more like pure torture."

"He's going to get me in big trouble," Nick fumed.

"Get *you* in trouble!" Soozie cried. "What about me? He—if he really isn't you—is threatening to expose my deepest secrets all over this campus. . . ." Soozie cut herself off. "Oh, forget I even said that. How in the world does this affect you . . . *if* you're telling the truth?"

"Because he's impersonating me. *You* think I'm guilty. Other people will, too." The waitress walked up and Nick stopped talking. As soon as she left with their order, he went on. "Whoever's behind this is trying to scare you off the Usenet. That's bad for the whole system. People have to trust it, or they'll stop using it and the university will shut down the chat rooms."

"Maybe they should." Soozie pouted and drank some soda. "You haven't heard half of it."

"So you'll stick around to tell me more?" Nick looked relieved.

Soozie didn't hesitate. "Maybe I'm nuts, but I think I believe you." Soozie told Nick about the late-night calls to Kappa. As Soozie revealed the details, Nick's expression changed from interested to incredulous to horrified. Nick O'Donnell was either a great actor or genuinely shocked and concerned.

"If this is a joke, whoever's doing this has one sick sense of humor," he remarked after Soozie finished.

"And not half your sense of poetry," Soozie said, a flirtatious note creeping into her voice.

"Did you like the poetry?" Nick began to smile.

"Loved it. And I loved your notes, really." Soozie bit her lip and looked down at her hands. "You know, if it weren't for this creepo hassling me on the Usenet, I'd say on-line dating has its advantages."

"So maybe sometime we can go on a real date."

"Sometime?" Soozie pretended to look offended. "What's wrong with now?" After casting an apologetic glance at Nancy, she suggested to

Nick, "Let's go somewhere quieter where we can really talk and get to know each other."

"Now, that would be more than terrific. I know just the spot," Nick said.

"He's asking for the check!" Holly cried, gripping Nancy's arm.

"Soozie, don't do this," Nancy murmured. The words were barely out of her mouth when Soozie got up and headed out of Anthony's, hand in hand with Nick.

"Is she crazy? Just because she knows him doesn't mean he's safe!" Holly exclaimed. "What do we do?"

Nancy was on her feet instantly. "Follow them." She tossed money down on the table and, without stopping to put on her coat, pushed her way through the crowd toward the exit and out into the parking lot. But Soozie and Nick were gone.

"Lost them!" Nancy sighed in frustration.

"Now what?" Holly asked. "She could be in big trouble."

Nancy shook her head. "Or not. We just don't know." Wind gusted across the lot and Nancy shivered. "Come on, let's go back inside, get our coats, then head for the Kappa house. With any luck, she'll come back there after her 'date.'" Nancy had to give the girl credit. Soozie had enough guts to stick around to ferret out the facts from Nick face-to-face. She only hoped Soozie hadn't trusted Nick too fast.

"Look who's here!" Holly exclaimed as they went down the short flight of steps leading back inside.

Nancy followed Holly's gaze across the crowded room. Jake sat alone at a table next to the waiters' station, near the kitchen. Nancy's heart flip-flopped.

Nancy started to go over to him when a waitress walked up to Jake. She tugged down her short leather mini and tossed her waist-length black hair off her face. Then she sat down.

Jake eyed the waitress appreciatively. Then he leaned forward and said something to her. She threw her head back and laughed.

Nancy's stomach did a somersault. She watched helplessly as Jake boldly flirted with another woman. "Let's get out of here," she said.

"What about Jake?" Holly said, motioning toward his table. The waitress, to Nancy's relief, was gone.

"I'll catch up with him later," Nancy said, masking her anger.

But she wondered if she should even bother.

Until now, Nancy had been sure their problems had to do with his not understanding her.

But as she headed for her car, she wondered if she knew the first thing about the *real* Jake Collins.

When Holly got back to the Kappa house, she headed straight for her room, where Jean-Marc was waiting for her.

"I'm back," Holly announced, tossing her coat and bag on the bed. Holly went over to the desk where Jean-Marc was keying something in on her computer.

He looked up at her and grinned. "Was Anthony's fun?"

"In a way," Holly said evasively. She and Nancy had decided to keep their plan with Soozie secret, at least until they saw if TDH even showed at the club.

She walked up behind him, looped her arms around his neck, and propped her chin on his head.

"What are you writing?"

She felt his shoulders tense up. He tapped some keys. The screen went blank. "Nothing."

"Nothing?" Holly asked skeptically as the modem whirred off.

Jean-Marc looked up guiltily. "Oh, well, something. Something personal."

"Oh," Holly said, sitting on his lap. "Should I be worried?"

Jean-Marc answered her with a kiss that took her breath away. After a few minutes she pulled away and ran her hand down the side of his face. "You won't get out of it that way, Jean-Marc."

"Out of what?" His blue eyes were innocent.

"Telling me what you were up to just now."

He shrugged. "Okay. I was just sending E-mail."

"E-mail?" Holly got up off his lap and propped her hip on the desk. "Who to?"

"Hey," Jean-Marc said, "no one that matters. It has nothing to do with me or you."

The defensive note in his voice took Holly off-guard. "If you're using my computer, it does," she countered, feeling a little confused. Why was Jean-Marc being so evasive?

"Holly," he added in a soft, sexy voice. "A guy's got to have some secrets. Remember one of the reasons you liked 'Flash' is that he was mysterious."

Holly's frown softened into a smile. "Flash" had been Jean-Marc's on-line screen name. "True," she admitted. "Even people in love are entitled to some privacy.

"By the way, Nancy came back with me from Anthony's. She's still here, downstairs. I thought we could nuke some popcorn and watch TV in the sunroom. Nancy's waiting for one of the other girls to get back from a date, and she might like company."

Jean-Marc checked his watch. "I can't hang around here much longer. I have to study."

Jean-Marc grabbed his jacket and headed for the door. Before Holly left the room, she kissed her finger, then touched the snapshot of her cat. Beneath the picture, Holly had posted the cat's name. "See ya later, Petals," she told the picture, then, turning out the light, she followed Jean-Marc downstairs.

Nancy stood in front of the fireplace in the Kappa common room warming her hands and listening to Soozie's description of her evening with Nick. Nancy was almost grateful for Soozie's problems. They kept her mind off her own.

"Nick and I went back to the computer center," Soozie told Nancy and Holly. "He needed to pick up some stuff. I decided to check my messages."

"Were there any?" Nancy asked.

"TDH has struck again," Soozie stated glumly, and handed a folded piece of paper to Nancy. "It wasn't from Nick, because it was sent at the very time we were all in Anthony's," she hurried to say.

"How do you know?" Nancy wondered.

Holly answered for Soozie. "E-mail always shows the time and date sent."

That should rule out Nick. Still, Nancy wondered. "Can't someone write a message and program the computer to send it later?"

"Yeah. I read about that, but I've never tried. It sounds complicated."

"You still think Nick is involved?" Soozie sounded shocked.

"Probably not, but he is pretty sophisticated when it comes to computers."

"Maybe, but I'm pretty smart when it comes to guys," Soozie said vehemently. "And Nick is *not* the bad TDH. Look at the message."

Nancy read the note aloud.

SSS—Are you trying to hide from me? You can't, you know. I know everything about you: your favorite nightshirt is pale blue. But no one on the Net cares about that. You stood me up in the chat room tonight. Now I have no choice but to reveal all. TDH

Holly started to giggle. She cast an apologetic look at Soozie. "Sorry. But that's a pretty wild threat. Posting the color of your nightgown on the campus Usenet."

"Really, Soozie, what does he mean by 'reveal all'?" Nancy laughed, too, but at the sight of Soozie's terrified face. "Sorry, Soozie; I know you're upset, but this threat pales by comparison to some of the others."

"Maybe to your way of thinking," Soozie replied, sounding miffed and looking distinctly uncomfortable.

"Nancy's got a point, though. That last message is more like the other weird stuff posted lately on the Usenet," Holly said.

"What weird stuff?" Soozie asked.

"All that time on-line, and you haven't noticed?" Holly looked skeptical.

"I've signed on only to check my E-mail and chat with TDH."

"Right. So you wouldn't have seen those messages about us Kappa sisters. Stuff about Leila's baking; the eyebrow job I flubbed; Janie's being a really tough person beneath that shy exterior. Whoever's posting that has a lot of inside info on what goes on in Kappa House."

"Oh, no!" Soozie's hands flew to her mouth.

"This is the first I've heard of it," Nancy commented.

"I never mentioned it because I didn't connect it with Soozie. Everyone thought it was a fraternity prank, at first, like those phone calls."

"The Zetas!" Nancy chorused with Holly, and laughed.

"What about the Zetas?" Janie asked, walking in. She stopped just inside the door and pulled some mail out of her cubbyhole.

"They've been posting some gems on the Usenet, about us Kappas. Haven't you noticed?" Holly asked. "You go on-line."

"Usually," Janie answered, "but I've got that performance coming up soon, and all my computer time is spent trying to work out the kinks in my video presentation." Turning to Soozie, Janie frowned. "You don't look so great."

"Same to you," Soozie said, but she sounded as if the life had been punched out of her.

"Soozie's on-line dating problems have taken a turn for the worse," Holly informed Janie.

"Not completely," Soozie said, some of the old spark returning as she spoke to Janie. "I met my on-line friend tonight. TDH truly is tall, dark, and handsome."

"You met Nick?" Janie looked stunned, then colored slightly and began stuffing her mail into her bag. "Uh—wasn't that really dangerous?"

"Not with Nancy and Holly looking over my shoulder to be sure he wasn't a psycho," Soozie said. "But," she continued with a soft smile, "he's anything but. I guess I was really wrong about the kind of guys you meet on-line."

"Patrons of the Wilder chat room will be glad to hear it has Sister Soozie's seal of approval," Janie said with some bitterness, then turned and left abruptly.

"More like certain patrons of the Wilder chat room are going to murder me," Soozie muttered.

"What did you just say?" Holly asked.

"Umm—look, guys, I've got something to tell you." Soozie threw her head back and stared at the ceiling. "You're really going to hate me for this. . . ."

"Now what you have done? I hope you aren't playing tricks on Janie again . . ." Holly started, but Nancy touched her arm.

"Soozie, does this have something to do with TDH's threat to reveal all?" Nancy asked quietly.

"I guess it's not a threat. He's been doing it all along." Soozie stared helplessly at Nancy, then blurted, "My diary. He stole my diary from my room."

"*Your diary!*" Holly exclaimed. "Are you for real, Soozie Beckerman? How could you write such garbage about your own sorority sisters, people who are supposed to be your friends?" Holly turned to Nancy, fuming. "Do you believe this? Now we know exactly where all those choice comments came from."

Soozie threw herself facedown on the sofa and began to sob. "I can't believe this is happening! I never expected anyone to see that diary."

"Look, Soozie," Holly said in disgust, "you've really blown it this time. And why didn't you tell us your diary was stolen?"

"Because I was embarrassed at the stuff TDH quoted in my E-mail. I was so scared he'd post my deepest secrets on the Usenet that it never occurred to me he'd use stuff about other girls." Soozie looked up, her makeup streaked with tears. "I sort of forgot what I had written. I feel awful."

Nancy and Holly exchanged an exasperated glance.

"You're not going to tell everyone, are you?" Soozie gasped to Holly. Then she shook her head in dismay. "But why not? In your shoes, I probably would."

"You're impossible, and whether I tell them or not, people are likely to figure it out, even if we don't stop TDH before he broadcasts exactly who the person is who 'has it in for the Kappas.' "

"You mean you're still going to help me?" Soozie looked from Holly to Nancy in disbelief.

"Look, part of being a Kappa is helping one another out of jams—no matter what," Holly said, sounding reluctant. "Sisters are supposed to support sisters. That's why I pledged this sorority."

"And that's why someday you'll make a terrific Kappa president," Soozie said through her tears. She reached for a tissue and delicately blew her nose, then added, "I don't deserve anyone's help, but I really didn't mean to hurt anyone."

Nancy didn't feel very sympathetic toward Soozie. But no one had a right to steal that diary, let alone post its contents. Nancy cleared her throat and asked, "Soozie, think. Have any strangers been hanging around here? Someone who might have had a chance to go up to your room and nose around?"

"People come and go all the time, men and women. People's friends and boyfriends. And during dinner the front of the sorority house is practically deserted," Soozie said plaintively. "Except at night, we never lock the door to the house. But who'd want to do this to me?"

Holly lifted her eyebrows but didn't comment.

"Actually, anyone who walked into this house the past week could be TDH," Nancy said.

"Nancy," Soozie pleaded, "please help me find this guy. Whoever he is has to be stopped."

"I'll try," Nancy promised. "But to be honest, right now, I have no idea how."

CHAPTER 10

Friday morning, Nancy woke up in a daze after having dreamt about Jake. She lay in bed a moment and wondered how her relationship with Jake had gone from terrific to terrible in only a few weeks. Jake's behavior with the waitress the night before still annoyed her, but he *had* just been flirting. She realized now exactly how he had felt when he saw her with Terry. Jealous, upset, and freaked over nothing.

A brisk shower and shampoo improved her mood slightly. She had no classes that day, so she dressed in a favorite pair of old jeans and the Emerson College sweatshirt Ned had given her. When she went to put on her makeup, she laughed at the sad face peering back at her from the mirror.

"Nancy Drew, are you losing it or what!" she told her reflection. However bad things were with Jake, it wasn't a major tragedy. What was the worst thing that could happen? They'd split up? She'd hurt, sure. And then—and then what? Nancy mused as she put on her lipstick. Why, she'd be on her own. Was that such a terrible thing? Since she started dating Ned in high school, she'd always had a guy in her life. After Ned, there was Peter, briefly, here at Wilder, then Jake. Exactly what *would* it feel like to be free— free to meet lots of other guys—or no one at all?

The thought scared her a little, but as she headed out of the dorm in search of Nick O'Donnell and the real TDH, her step was light.

She was pretty sure Nick wasn't the culprit, but whoever was knew enough about poetry and Nick's interest in it to impersonate him on-line.

She checked the computer lab in the basement of Graves Hall first. The student helper on duty said Nick had a literature seminar right upstairs.

Nancy arrived just as the seminar ended. She stood outside the door, letting the students file out of the classroom. Nick was still inside, his back to her, talking animatedly to a woman who looked as if she might be the professor.

A dark-haired girl in a long print skirt brushed by her. Nancy smiled in surprise. "Hi, Janie! I didn't know you took this class."

Clutching a pile of books, Janie turned around. "Nancy," she said, frowning briefly. "What are you doing here?"

"Looking for someone," Nancy replied, noticing that Janie's usually creamy complexion was blotchy, and her big eyes had dark circles beneath them.

"Oh, well, I can't stay and talk right now," Janie said. "I have to go to the language lab. I've got to tutor a sophomore in French."

Nancy watched Janie go down the stairs and something clicked at the back of her mind. Janie had said something about Soozie and TDH last night that bothered Nancy. But at the moment she couldn't remember what. Before she could give it another thought, Nick emerged from the classroom. "Nick?"

He turned and gave her a puzzled smile. "Do we know each other?"

"Yes and no," Nancy said, and introduced herself. She studied him carefully as she spoke. He had frank, honest eyes and a solid, earthy quality. He didn't look like the sort of devious person who would enjoy scaring Soozie out of her wits. But Nancy knew looks could be deceiving, so she tried to keep an open mind about Nick. "I saw you last night with Soozie, in Anthony's," she told him.

Recognition dawned on Nick's face. "Oh, you're one of her bodyguards," he joked.

Nancy had to laugh. "You could put it that way. I'm glad we weren't needed. Could I talk to you a minute? I'm still trying to track down the 'other' TDH. I think he's tied in with prank calls at the dorm and other nasty stuff posted on the Usenet."

"Good luck. This guy should be stopped, whoever he is. But how can *I* help?"

The hall was crowded, and Nancy motioned Nick over to one of the windows. She sat on the sill, and he sat next to her. "What class was that, by the way?"

"Modern poetry. This month, the seminar is built around the confessional poets—Anne Sexton, Elizabeth Bishop, Robert Lowell . . ."

"Sylvia Plath!" Nancy supplied. The book she had seen on the coffee table in the Kappa common room the other day was a copy of Sylvia Plath's poems. It was one of the books, she realized now, that Janie had picked up on her way out of the sorority house.

"Yes, Plath and Lowell are the most famous of that group. But we're also studying some of the lesser-known poets. Those are the ones I quoted."

Nancy took that in. Then she changed direction. "You're a computer expert. How could someone impersonate you on the Usenet?"

"It would be easy enough if you knew our screen names. Whoever it is knew Soozie's handle, and somehow found out mine, maybe by lurking in a chat room. And anyone could find her E-mail address. It's listed in the university on-line address database."

"So the only way to know who sent the message is to trace it back to its source," Nancy said. "That sounds doable."

"Not unless you're some kind of super hacker.

I have no idea how to trace a message back to where it came from, even assuming it was someone using Wilder's system. People can tap into the Usenet from virtually anywhere."

Nancy stared bleakly at Nick. "In the world?"

"That's the problem. But, Nancy," Nick said encouragingly, "I'm not a hacker. There are probably ways I know nothing about to trace messages. But I'll help in any way I can. I like Soozie, and I hate that someone's trying to hurt her."

Nancy remembered something. "Nick, how well do you know Janie Covington?"

"Who?" Nick asked, puzzled. Then, slowly, recognition dawned on his face. "Right, Janie. The skinny girl with the long skirt. She's in my seminar. You were talking to her in the hall just now."

"Yes," Nancy said.

"Barely. I never knew her last name until you mentioned it. Why do you ask?"

"I thought you guys might be friends," Nancy replied.

After saying goodbye to Nick, Nancy went to the nearest pay phone. She rang Holly at the sorority and they agreed to meet after Holly's drawing class that afternoon to discuss their next step to find TDH.

By the time Nancy left Graves Hall, she had a strong hunch who was tormenting Soozie, but no way to prove it.

*   *   *

"Montana, don't you have something better to do than pester me?" Eileen moaned, tossing a navy blue shirt in the pile of white wash.

Even holed up in her room in suite 301 at Thayer Hall, sorting her laundry, Eileen wasn't safe. Somehow in the middle of the day, when everyone should be at class, Montana, Kara Verbeck, and Nikki Bennett had found her.

Montana's latest phase in her obsession with Ray Johansson involved promoting his career. Now she was determined to have Radical Moves perform at Club Z.

Montana retrieved the blue shirt and put it with the dark clothes. "What's better than helping a friend climb the ladder of success?"

"Probably getting him to climb a ladder to your room some night and ask you to elope!" Eileen quipped.

"That's a thought!" Montana said brightly. "But unfortunately, Ray is slow on the uptake. So I'd better concentrate on what matters most to him these days—his music, not me."

"I've told you one hundred times," Eileen cried, exasperated, "I've got no say when it comes to Jason's bookings for his club. It's not like I'm his booking agent or something."

Montana positioned herself with her back against Eileen's door and tapped her foot. She was determined, as usual, to get her way. "And I heard you. I'm not asking you to ask Jason to book Ray, am I?" Montana turned to Kara and Nikki.

"No," Kara said, her sea green eyes wide. "All Montana wants is for you to be sure Jason tunes in to our radio program tonight. Ray's granting us an on-air live interview."

"With one of the other members of his band," Nikki added.

"You know how he loves to talk about music," Montana reminded Eileen.

"That's great, but what does this have to do with me? Short of luring Jason into his office, locking the door, and jamming my Walkman over his ears, I don't see how I can *make* him listen to your show."

"Sounds like a good idea to me," Kara said, giggling.

"Get serious, Eileen," Montana said. "Just tell Jason that Ray is really hot. Once he hears Radical Moves on the air tonight, he'll be dying to have the band debut in his club."

"And there's something else Montana forgot to mention," Kara said. "Ray's given us a demo tape of two songs never played in public before. This is the first time Radical Moves will be heard since the group re-formed. How can you let Jason miss that?"

"Beats me," Eileen said, sidling toward the door. The three other women were driving her nuts. Emmet felt uncomfortable getting involved with Jason's business at Club Z. But even if he didn't, Eileen did not want to get involved with Montana and her obvious machinations to win

Ray's heart. "But if I see him, I'll see what I can do," she said evasively. "Now I have to run."

"I thought you were doing laundry," Montana said, trying to block Eileen's path.

"I was. But thanks to you guys, it's too late. I've got a meeting with"—Eileen blurted the first thing that came to her head—"my freshman advisor. Catch you all later."

"Jonathan Baur has sunk to new depths—or risen to new heights—of horror," Stephanie told Casey as they sat over espresso at Java Joe's. "I haven't decided which yet."

"What happened now? It must have been pretty bad for you to leave work early once again," Casey said.

"I was doing a makeover for a customer when he walked up and said he had to speak to me. Then he took me aside and told me my own makeup was too extreme for Berrigan's dress code."

"So you just left?"

"Yes. Right then. I left the woman with cream on one half of her face and walked out the door, saying I suddenly felt sick—and I do. Sick of Jonathan," she said, with a defiant toss of her head.

"Don't you wish," Casey chided.

Stephanie shrugged. "Who am I kidding? I feel as if a truck ran over my heart. What can I do?"

"Get your act together, Stephanie."

A snide reply died on Stephanie's lips. "How? I mean, I'm trying. I haven't looked at another guy in a week. But Jonathan doesn't know that and won't give me a chance to convince him I'm a reformed person."

Stephanie saw the skepticism written all over Casey's face. "You don't believe me either, do you?"

Casey hesitated. "I think I do. I think you want to reform, but, Stephanie, can you?"

"Yes," Stephanie said firmly. "I can, and I have. Life without Jonathan is the pits." Stephanie studied her hands.

"Don't look so hopeless," Casey said.

"Easy for you to say," Stephanie responded tersely. "Getting Jonathan to even look at me again is going to take a major miracle."

"Miracles aren't in my department. But brainstorming is. I just have to know that if I help you, you're really going to try to make it work this time. Because I can't take one more round of you carrying on like a lovesick moose."

"A what?" Stephanie cried, insulted.

Casey laughed. "Forget it—bad image. The point is, if you really try to mend your ways, I think I might be able to help you get Mr. Perfect eating from the palm of your hand again."

"Sounds good," Stephanie said, feeling the first stirrings of hope. "But all I want is for him to know I mean it when I say I love him."

"That's the spirit," Casey congratulated her. Then she motioned for Stephanie to come closer. In a soft voice, she began.

"Okay. Promise to do just what I tell you." Casey's big eyes twinkled. "Here's my plan. . . ."

CHAPTER 11

Nancy blew her hair out of her eyes and started up the steps to the second floor of the Kaplan Center. Holly's painting studio was in the front of the building, and Nancy hoped Holly's studiomate wouldn't be around to interfere with their conversation.

"Nancy!" Holly greeted her warmly as Nancy poked her head in the door. The studio was bright with late-afternoon light, and Holly's big, colorful paintings lifted Nancy's spirits.

Nancy settled down in an overstuffed easy chair and draped her legs over the frayed upholstered arms. "Did you report the crank calls to the phone company?" she asked, accepting a chilled bottle of water from Holly.

"Yes, for all the good it did," Holly answered. "They gave me a code to punch in as soon as we get the next crank call. Phone company computers have tracking programs now. But whoever was calling stopped."

"No calls last night?" Nancy asked.

"No. And then I found out it's virtually impossible to trace calls on the Internet back to their source via the phones."

Nancy threw her hands up. "Every idea we have seems to hit a brick wall."

"Not quite," Holly said. "This guy also told me a couple of interesting things. He said that *if* the person harassing Soozie on-line and through her E-mail was hooked into a Wilder U account and not using one of the commercial service providers on the Internet, then the phone records actually might help. Though we'd have to check hundreds of calls from when Soozie's bad messages started."

Nancy took heart. "That was just a couple of days ago."

"He also told me that if we knew a real computer whiz, that person might be able to trace the calls back to whoever sent them, some other way." Holly shrugged. "But to tell you the truth, I couldn't follow half of what he told me."

"Join the crowd," Nancy admitted. "I feel really out of my element here, and I'm beginning to think I'd better bone up on how to navigate my way around cyberspace fast. Meanwhile, I know someone who knows everything about this stuff."

"Well, we need all the help we can get."

"I'm going to call her now." Then Nancy remembered something. "Holly, we know that

Nick's handle is TDH and Soozie's is SSS, but who else knew that?"

"Let me think." Holly closed her eyes. "Bess. Now I remember, it was Bess. She came over to Kappa with Casey and told a bunch of sisters that Soozie was going on-line."

"So that means Bess, Casey, you—" Nancy ticked off names on her fingers. "Anyone else?"

"Maybe Darcy, but I'm not sure. We were all hanging out watching soaps in the sunroom. Come to think of it, a lot of people were around."

"How about Janie?"

Holly nodded vigorously. "Yes, Janie was there, too."

I knew it, Nancy congratulated herself. Janie must have known who TDH was from the start. The other night Janie had known TDH was Nick, even though no one else had mentioned his name in connection with Soozie—at least not in front of Janie. However, Nancy decided not to share her suspicions with Holly until she had more proof.

"Nancy," Holly asked warily, "don't tell me you think another Kappa had something to do with this?"

"I wouldn't rule it out," Nancy said cautiously.

"But how? I mean how could one of us call ourselves?"

"Easy. Everyone has her own phone in her own room. It would be easy to call the house phone."

"Of course," Holly said sadly. "I just hate to think it's some inside prankster. Though I suppose that's better than picturing a psycho out there ready to do Soozie some real bodily harm."

Holly had a point. But Nancy wasn't ready to rule out the possibility of Soozie's being in real danger. Soozie might be popular with some Kappa sisters, but others hated her. Someone could crack and really hurt her.

Nancy tried to figure out exactly what to do next. "Let's phone Soozie at Kappa and have her bring along the printouts of her messages tonight. Meanwhile I'm going to phone Reva. She's practically a genius when it comes to computers."

"Will she help us? This is going to take some time," Holly warned Nancy.

"Reva will jump at the chance to solve a thorny computer problem. In fact," she added with the first real laugh she'd had in days, "Reva will probably think it's fun."

Ginny collapsed in a booth in the Bumblebee Diner. She had pulled a double shift at the hospital. Her feet were killing her, and her stomach was so empty it ached.

"Ginny?"

At the sound of Ray's voice, her exhaustion vanished. "Ray?" she said, turning around, a big smile on her face.

Ray flashed a quick, nervous grin. One look behind him and Ginny's smile dimmed. He was with a skinny girl with an ordinary face, short shaggy hair, and amazing blue eyes. She wore a small tattoo on the back of her wrist and lots of heavy makeup.

"Umm, Ginny," Ray said, putting his hand on Karin's back and pushing her toward Ginny's booth. "This is Karin Messer. She's the new vocalist in Radical Moves."

"Ray's new band," Karin purred. She lifted her eyes toward Ray and gave him an adoring look. Ginny's stomach turned.

Her dismay must have shown because Ray suddenly blushed. "And, um, this is Ginny Yuen, my . . . umm . . ."

"A friend," Ginny said coolly, and shook Karin's hand. "I heard you and Ray being interviewed on Montana's show tonight," Ginny said, trying to keep her voice even. "I caught the whole thing on a radio in the hospital."

Karin looked blankly at Ginny.

"I'm a volunteer there," Ginny explained, and noticed Karin wore rings on every finger but her thumbs.

"Oh," Karin said, putting her hand on Ray's shoulder. Ray jerked back as if stung. Ginny considered him carefully. He didn't just look uncomfortable, he looked really upset.

"It sounded like you guys have known each other for years," Ginny said, keeping her eyes on Ray.

"We haven't," Ray blurted. "You know that."

"But it's cool that people out there in radio land think so," Karin said, leaning into Ray's shoulder. "Fans are so curious about how the man-woman thing works out between members of a band," she said.

Ray made a face. "Not the real fans who listen because they love the music," he said tightly. He cast a pleading look at Ginny.

What's going on? she wondered. Was he dating this girl or not? Ginny studied Ray. She had no idea if he and Karin were dating, but at the moment he looked as if he wished Karin would just get lost.

Ray was too kind a person to say so outright, but Karin didn't seem to have a clue. She hooked her arm through Ray's and said, "So, are we going to eat here?" She made as if she was going to sit down across from Ginny.

To Ginny's relief, Ray stopped her. "I have a better idea. Let's go over to Anthony's and take in the last set. We can eat while we listen."

"Fine by me." Karin smiled and said goodbye to Ginny.

Ray sent Ginny a pleading look, then followed Karin out of the diner.

Ginny watched them leave, feeling that Ray had just taken another little bit of her heart with him.

The waitress brought her food, but Ginny had lost her appetite. She sat back and stared glumly at her french fries.

Her mind told her that she should be moving on, looking for a new guy. But her heart said something totally different.

* * *

Right after dinner, Nancy went directly to Graves Hall to meet Reva, who was already there with Holly and Soozie.

"You got my message!" Nancy declared, walking up.

"You bet," Reva said, her dark eyes bright in anticipation. "Holly just filled me in on what's been going on."

"It's sure one big mess," Soozie remarked in a subdued voice.

"Anyway," Reva continued, "since the threatening notes came over Soozie's E-mail and not just on-line in the chat rooms, I'm not sure why you need me to solve the problem," she added as the four girls trooped down the stairs.

"Because none of *us* knows enough to figure out what's going on," Soozie admitted with a tight laugh. "If *I* did, I would have solved this whole mystery myself and saved my reputation at the same time."

"It's not just *your* reputation that's on the line here, Soozie," Holly reminded her. "Half of Kappa has been mentioned on the Net. But there's no point wasting time worrying about that now. Let's just see if we can put an end to TDH's postings."

"Better yet, an end to TDH," Soozie joked grimly, and Nancy had to laugh.

They walked into the computer room. "Oh," Soozie said, "Nick's not here tonight." She sounded disappointed.

"Too bad," Holly said. "He might have been helpful."

Nancy turned to Reva. "What did you mean when you said we didn't need you?"

Reva led them to an empty computer station and sat down. As she punched in her password to get into the system, she told Nancy, "Because if someone's been sending Soozie weird E-mail, then the address should be right on it."

"What address?" Soozie sounded confused.

"Why, the sender's, of course," Reva said.

"You mean we could have figured out who wrote the messages just from looking at them?" Nancy had trouble believing that. She had looked over some of the mail pretty carefully. She couldn't remember seeing anyone's name—except the initials TDH—at the end of each letter.

"I'll show you." Reva reached out for the copies of Soozie's correspondence. Soozie handed them over reluctantly.

"I'm getting sick of *everyone's* reading my personal stuff," she grumbled.

Reva was checking the printouts. Her expression when she looked up to meet Nancy's eyes was a mixture of respect and annoyance. "Whoever did this is no computer newbie."

"What's the problem?" Soozie asked, drumming her fingers against the partition between their terminal and the next one.

"All your E-mail comes from NODL@Wilder.-edu," Reva said, reading the address aloud.

Soozie puckered her forehead. "N-O-D-L,"

Soozie said aloud. "Why, those are Nick's initials. . . ." She swallowed visibly. "That means he did send every single message. The rotten ones, too."

"No, that's not what it means. Not necessarily," Reva said. Then she asked Soozie to call up the file with her E-mail. "I want to check this out on the screen."

Reva explained that every piece of E-mail sent has the sender's address. "But there's a command that overrides the real name of the sender so you could substitute a fake name. So, say, Nancy, that you punch in my name and send something to Andy—it'll look like the message came from me, not you."

"Is that legal?" Nancy asked.

"Hard to tell," Reva said. "The law is very fuzzy when it comes to E-mail and the Internet."

"But that means you have no way of knowing where it came from." Holly sounded really upset.

"That makes it easy for the phantom TDH to cover his tracks." Once again Nancy felt thwarted. "So we're dealing with an experienced hacker here."

"Not necessarily. Just someone who definitely knows more than your average Wilder network user," Reva said.

"So now what do we do?" Holly asked. "Give up?"

"No way." Reva rubbed her palms together gleefully. "The fun's just started. There are ways to track messages. At least to the general domain. . . ." She laughed at the expressions on their faces. "That means the part of the university system the messages came from. Because *if* there is more than one TDH, we'll be able to see that the messages have at least two different origins."

Reva turned back to the keyboard and after a second was totally engrossed in tapping out numbers and retrieving E-mail files.

"All right!" Reva's exclamation jolted Nancy right back to the present.

"You found something!" Nancy said, jumping up.

Reva nodded and turned to Soozie. "TDH is definitely two different people, at least. And so your Nick could be in the clear."

"Great," Holly said.

Soozie beamed at Holly. Holly beamed back.

"I just want to double-check these messages." Reva had sorted out Soozie's printouts and was comparing them with files on the screen. Nancy noticed the screen files had all sorts of coded gibberish running across the top. "See this first group of numbers on the top of this message? It's an account number. That means it came from one site, and I think . . ." Reva paused to figure something out. "This number means the message came from one of the machines in this lab."

"Was Nick here that first night?" Nancy asked.

"I'm not sure. I mean, he was here when I signed on," Soozie said.

"He probably watched you choose your handle," Reva said.

"Yes, he must have," Soozie said. "Before I chased him away."

"He also knew she was blond and a Kappa," Holly stated. "He had seen her in person."

"Then," Nancy said, suddenly able to piece the puzzle together, "he must have gone to another machine and chatted with you your first time on-line."

"Look at this," Reva said. "All these sick messages have some coding in common. I wonder . . ." Reva paused and checked a copy of the Wilder U student computer handbook she'd brought with her. "Oh, no!" Reva gasped, and quickly went back to her keyboard. "I don't believe this!"

She looked from Soozie to Holly and finally to Nancy. "All the weirdo threats have the same account code in common. It's a Kappa account."

"A Kappa account?" Holly repeated. "What's that mean?"

"Does that have something to do with our E-mail addresses?" Soozie asked. "Like mine is Sbeck@kappa.wilder.edu."

"Right. Kappa has its own domain—or sub-address—on the university system," Reva told them. "I forgot. Andy told me that last year the university launched a pilot program where eventually all the dorms and other residences, like the frat and sorority houses, will have their own sub-addresses. Kappa and Alpha Delt, along with two of the dorms, were among the group selected as test sites."

Slowly the meaning of Reva's discovery dawned on Nancy. "So TDH turns out to be a Kappa after all."

Holly's and Soozie's faces registered pure shock.

But Nancy could barely suppress her smile. "And I have a very good idea exactly which sister was out to get Soozie." She paused, then announced her conclusion: "Janie."

"Janie Covington?" Holly looked stunned.

"Of course. She hates me!" Soozie exclaimed angrily.

"But are you sure, Nancy?" Holly asked, still incredulous. "One of the diary entries posted on the Net was about Janie. Why would she post a remark about herself?"

"What exactly did it say?" Soozie asked in a subdued voice.

"Something like she was shy and sweet outside, tough inside . . . I don't remember the exact words," Holly said.

"But," Soozie admitted hesitantly, "I wrote much worse about Janie than that."

Nancy thought a moment, then said, "Listen, guys. I've got it. If Janie's smart enough to work the computer angle, she's definitely smart enough to cover her tracks. She posted a diary entry about herself."

"So no one would suspect her," Holly added.

"Right. And everything so far points to her. She takes the same poetry seminar as Nick—"

"She does?" Soozie interrupted.

Nancy nodded. "So she can quote the same kind of poems—or knows enough about the poets to copy their style when she wrote those threats. Maybe she has a crush on Nick," Nancy said.

"I didn't even know she knew him," Soozie said. "But that must be her 'mystery guy,' the one she was talking to Bess about earlier this week."

"The one she didn't have nerve to ask out," Holly remembered. 'So she must be jealous of Soozie."

"But I didn't know Nick was TDH until last night. The spooky messages, the threats, the diary postings—they all happened before I met Nick. How did she figure out it was him?" Soozie inquired.

"I'm not sure," Nancy admitted, "but she knew that you met Nick last night." Nancy reminded the other girls about Janie's reaction to Soozie's meeting TDH in person. "She knew Nick's name, but no one had mentioned him by name in front of her. And then, of course, she lives at Kappa and—"

"Lives at Kappa?" Soozie repeated. "Janie doesn't live at Kappa. That's what our last major fight was about. I told her one of us had to leave the sorority. So she moved out."

"Janie lives off campus," Holly stated.

Nancy stared woefully at Holly and felt as if she had just walked smack into a big brick wall.

CHAPTER 12

"Y̶ou sure don't look convinced," Holly told Nancy. "But it's the truth. Janie doesn't live at Kappa anymore."

"I hear you," Nancy said, and retreated behind a frown.

"And you're sure the messages can be traced to Kappa?" Soozie asked Reva.

"No doubt about it. But I want to dig in deeper. Let's see if I can get down to another level of information."

Holly had no idea what Reva was up to; she wished that whatever information had made Reva decide a Kappa was the culprit would prove to be wrong. But her instincts told her Reva was right. Several sisters hated Soozie's guts. Even she had been almost glad to hear at first that Soozie was the victim of some kind of dirty trick.

Now, thinking about her own reactions to Soozie's predicament, Holly felt definite pangs of guilt.

"Well, one thing's for sure," Reva suddenly said. "I've traced every threatening message down to one single account."

"Whose?" Holly, Nancy, and Soozie asked in unison.

"That's trickier to find out because the real name has been bypassed, but maybe if I can access every Kappa's E-mail, then I can find out who belongs to which number here." Reva stopped talking and went back to punching keys.

"Now we're cooking!" Reva declared a few minutes later. "I've found a slew of messages posted a few weeks back. And they have the same account number as the phoney TDH's. With any luck, the person will sign it with a handle, or the correct address will clue us in to the sender." After a few more keystrokes, a short note appeared on the screen.

Nancy and Soozie leaned over Reva's shoulder, blocking Holly's view for a moment.

"Who in the world is Blondie?" Nancy asked.

Soozie whirled around, her blue eyes dark with fury. "Holly Thornton, that's *you!*"

"The night's still young," Ray told Cory and Austin as the two men headed for the door of Ray's dorm room. "It's Friday. No one will mind if we jam here on a weekend." He motioned toward his bongo drums and an extra guitar leaning against the wall.

Austin, Cory, and Karin had gathered in Ray's room to celebrate Ray and Karin's interview on WLDR Talk Radio with Montana, Karin, and Nikki. It had gone well, and Cory in particular had been more than enthusiastic about the two new songs Montana had played on the air.

"I'm ready to call it a night," Austin finally told Ray, not quite meeting Ray's eyes. Ray wished he'd stay. Ever since they'd met at Ray's after dinner, Austin had been shooting dirty looks at Karin. On the air earlier she had suggested to the audience that she and Ray were a hot item on- and *off*stage.

With that the two guys left. Ray stood in the doorway, while Karin put on her jacket. "It's been real," Karin said, brushing against him as she headed out the door. He was surprised she didn't linger.

Ray debated with himself for a moment. He didn't like the idea of being in his room with a woman who had a one-sided crush on him. But he needed to talk things out with Karin before tensions in the band got much worse.

"Karin," he called after her as she started down the hall. "Got a minute?"

Karin's eyebrows shot up. "Sure. I'm free these days. In case *you* hadn't noticed." There was a sad tone in her voice.

Ray beckoned her back into his room. He left the door open a crack and motioned for her to sit down.

"What's up?" she asked. And suddenly he realized she wasn't flirting.

"Us," he said. Her thick, dark eyebrows shot up. "Or rather what you seem to be doing when we're around other people together. Like Montana, or my friend Ginny, or, worst of all, Austin."

"What am I doing?"

Ray swallowed hard. Had he read her wrong?

"You're flirting," he said directly. "And though you're a wonderful person and I think we'll be friends, I have to tell you that I'm not interested."

Karin shifted in her seat. "Ray—I'd better explain—"

He interrupted. "Wait. There's something else I have to say. Whatever you're doing, stop doing it in front of Austin. He's beginning to freak. That's pretty obvious these days. He's getting jealous."

"Not jealous enough," Karin interjected, then flashed Ray a sheepish smile. "He should be," she said, her blue eyes sparkling, "you're a pretty cool guy. A girl could really get to like you."

"Not a good idea," Ray said gently but firmly. "I'm not available."

"So you've said."

"Look, I've already lost one band to jealousies and rivalries and all sorts of nasty stuff. I have no intention of having Radical Moves break up because Austin thinks you and I are involved. You're an awesome singer, and together we give

Radical Moves a dynamite new sound. But I'd rather have you leave the band now than have you ruin what already exists with Austin, Cory, and me."

Karin toyed with one of her rings before speaking. "I'll spell it out for you, Ray. When I decided to give Radical Moves a try, I thought at first that dealing with Austin would be doable. But playing with him every day, even though he's acting cold, I realized I still loved him."

"You do?" Ray hadn't even thought of that possibility.

Karin shoved her thick, shaggy bangs off her face and gave an embarrassed little smile. "Wow, this is pretty awkward. You know, when I first joined the band, I thought if I got Austin jealous, maybe he'd try to win me back. I used you to try to get at him. I don't blame you if you're mad. I'm sorry."

Ray couldn't believe what he was hearing. "You were faking it?"

"You could put it that way," Karin admitted.

"I can't say I'm happy about this—the being used part," Ray added, annoyed. "And I am mad, but forget it. I'll get over it." After a minute, he added. "I know only one thing. You'd better stop acting as if we're a couple, because we aren't." And never will be, he added to himself.

Karin zipped her jacket and started for the hall. "I don't know if you want advice," Ray said as she was leaving, "but here goes: I think you should just tell Austin you want to get back with him."

"Just like that!" Karin snapped her fingers and gave a short, sarcastic laugh. "As if he'd listen."

"You'll never know unless you try. But all I care about is the band. You have to make some kind of decision. Is your commitment to the band or to Austin? If Austin decides he doesn't want to get back together, do you still want to stay with the band?"

Karin didn't even stop to think. "Absolutely. Music comes first for me, Ray. Just like for you."

Ray relaxed and began to smile. "Great. I was hoping you'd say that. Now as for Austin, one last hint here. Take it slow with him. Maybe try to heal those old wounds before either of you starts to make new ones."

"I'll think about that, Ray," Karin said. "And thanks," she added, then reached up and pecked his cheek. It was a friendly kiss that made Ray feel things just might be okay now between them.

Nancy turned to Holly, unable to believe what she'd just heard. "You're Blondie?" Holly Thornton was the last person in the world she'd suspect of harassing anyone.

"Yes, but—" Holly tried to protest.

"But what?" Soozie said with a sneer. "Come to think of it, you were the one ready to give up just now, when Reva hit the first snag."

"Stop it, Soozie," Holly cried, putting her hands over her ears. "I won't listen to this."

Just then the systems administrator on duty that evening came over. "Hey, ladies, you're disturbing people. Either pipe down or take your argument outside, okay?"

"Good idea," Reva said, flashing Nancy a warning look. Reva gathered together the printouts and her notes. "There's no reason for us to stay here now."

Outside, Holly turned on Soozie. "Why would I do that to you?"

Soozie eyed Holly scornfully. "You've totally ruined my reputation with the Kappas by publishing my diary on-line. You've humiliated me. Now you'll have no serious rival when you run for Kappa president next year. That's reason enough. Maybe just because you hate me, like half the other Kappas."

"So half the other Kappas could have done this," Holly countered, suddenly feeling cornered.

"But not on your machine," Nancy said quietly. Nancy's heart ached as she watched Holly's face drop.

"What can I do to convince you it wasn't me?" Holly looked pleadingly at Reva.

Reva shook her head. "I'll think it through more carefully. Maybe there's some angle we overlooked. But as far as I can tell, those messages came through your account, Holly."

Nancy's ears perked up. "Her account?" She tried to review everything she'd learned about computers, including what Reva had told her to-night. "Holly, who else uses your computer?"

Holly shrugged and didn't answer.

Nancy frowned. Holly was holding something back. "Holly, whatever's going on here is serious. What do you know that you're not telling us?"

"Nothing," Holly insisted.

Nancy softened her tone. "Look, I don't believe you're capable of hurting Soozie or anyone this way. But I think you know something about what's going on here. Whatever you're holding back is only going to make things worse." Nancy's words hung in the air.

Holly let out a sharp breath. "Okay. Someone else does use my machine—Jean-Marc."

"He's TDH?" Soozie cried. "That jerk, why—"

Nancy interrupted. "Stop, Soozie. Let Holly finish." She was beginning to understand exactly why Soozie could drive someone to a life of crime.

"When we left Anthony's and came back to Kappa the other night, he was upstairs in my room. I had told him he could use my computer to write a paper. Anyway, when I came in, he hid whatever he was writing. Then he told me it was E-mail. But he wouldn't tell me whom he sent it to." Holly's voice broke slightly. "I mean, I can't believe he'd do this to anyone."

"But you haven't known him long," Reva pointed out gently. "And you did meet him over the Usenet. Is he good with computers?"

"Great," Holly admitted ruefully. "He's thinking of majoring in computer science."

"That's it. I'm calling the police in now," Soozie said threateningly. "That creep has had it in for me ever since I told you to be careful when it came to dating someone on-line. I said you'd meet a loser, and now look what's you've done. *Your* loser has just about ruined my life."

"Soozie, just cool it," Nancy warned, getting annoyed. "You're not helping." Soozie shut her mouth but continued to glare at Holly. Soozie could glare all she wanted—Nancy didn't care. She needed to find out exactly what Jean-Marc was up to. He sounded like the perfect suspect. Though something about him niggled at the back of Nancy's mind, something that didn't quite fit in with the details of Soozie's story.

"Holly, where is he now?" Nancy asked.

"At Kappa. In my room. We're supposed to have a late dinner over at the diner."

Nancy avoided Holly's eyes and started down the walk. "We'd better get back to Kappa now. I have a hunch that if he's our man, we might actually catch him in the act. He knows Soozie is at the computer center. He might be posting messages to her even as we speak."

In her room in Jamison Hall, Bess lay curled up in her bed. Pain mixed with anger and with feelings she had no name for. A lump rose to her throat, and she broke down. Since she had been back in her dorm room, all she'd been able to do was cry.

Bess was glad her roommate, Leslie King, had left already for the weekend. Or would it be better if Leslie were around? Bess wondered now if she'd survive the weekend alone. She knew she could set up another appointment with her counselor, Victoria Linden, but Bess sometimes had trouble telling Vicky what she was feeling. But then, Bess was having trouble in general with her feelings. They felt all bottled up in her chest. If she let them out, they would grow big and powerful and threaten to take over her life.

But there was one person she knew she really could talk to. It had worked before, a couple of weeks ago in River Heights. Shakily, she reached for the phone and dialed.

Even as it began to ring at the other end, Bess broke down again. She was crying so hard that when someone picked up the receiver, she couldn't speak right away.

"Hello?" the voice said. "Hello?"

There was a silence, then the voice asked, "Is anyone there?"

Finally, Bess managed to gasp through her tears. "Don't hang up. Oh, please," she sobbed into the mouthpiece. "I really need to talk to you. Oh, Ned . . ."

CHAPTER 13

When Nancy and the other girls arrived back at the sorority, the logs in the fireplace of the Kappa common room had burned down to embers. Nancy headed straight for the staircase, wondering if they'd find Jean-Marc in Holly's room. She hoped he'd still be there, possibly posting E-mail under Nick's name.

"My room's at the top of the stairs," Holly told Nancy and Reva. Soozie already was charging ahead.

Holly stopped Soozie and Reva at the top of the steps. Light seeped out from under her door. Either Jean-Marc was gone and had left the lights on, or he was still there. "What now?" she asked Nancy.

Nancy squeezed Holly's arm. "Now we find out the truth." Nancy shoved open the door. All four girls crowded through the entrance at once.

Jean-Marc looked up from Holly's computer.

161

"Hello?" he said, startled. Then he spotted Holly bringing up the rear. His surprise gave way to a smile. "Back at last," he said.

Nancy positioned herself near Holly's computer and motioned Reva to follow suit. She didn't want to give him a chance to erase anything crucial.

"Jean-Marc," Holly said. "This is Nancy."

"Hi," he said amiably.

"There's a problem with Holly's computer account," Nancy said cautiously.

"The computer seems to be working fine," he said. His hand inched toward the keyboard. Quickly, Nancy grabbed it. "Sorry," she said, gripping it firmly, "but why don't you step away from that desk."

"What is going on here?" he asked, baffled.

"Nancy will explain," Holly said weakly.

"Soozie's being hassled through her E-mail," Nancy said.

"So I've heard." He glanced at Soozie. "Just when we all convinced you to go on-line. Sometimes weird people surf the Net. It's not such a big deal."

"It can be," Reva said angrily. "Soozie's threats came from Holly's account."

Jean-Marc gasped. "Holly? You?"

"Not me," she said.

"You think I have something to do with this?" Jean-Marc looked stupefied.

"Maybe, maybe not," Nancy said. "What were you doing just now?"

"Or last night, when you were sending E-mail," Holly chimed in. "Whom were you writing to?"

Jean-Marc's cheeks reddened. "That was private."

"If you're innocent, you'd better tell what you were really doing," Holly pleaded, taking his hand.

He pulled away. "Okay. Look, then." He started toward the keyboard, but Reva stopped him.

"Just tell me how to get into the file," Reva said in a firm but soft voice. Jean-Marc gave her the information, then stalked away.

Nancy crowded around the screen, along with Soozie and Reva. Holly hung behind, afraid to look.

"What's this?" Soozie exclaimed.

Nancy read the first letter. It had nothing to do with SSS. It was a note defending the joys of on-line dating.

Reva called up an earlier letter. Nancy had to smile as she read it. "I'd say that Jean-Marc has his own little project going here." Nancy turned to Jean-Marc. "I guess we owe you an apology."

Jean-Marc shrugged, looking a little hurt. "I didn't mean to make anyone suspicious," he said. "But I thought it might be fun to create a site, a channel, for people to talk about their experiences making friends through the Wilder Usenet."

Nancy pushed Holly toward the monitor. "It seems Jean-Marc thinks that the dangers of on-line dating are greatly exaggerated. And that he met the girl of his dreams through the Usenet and thinks everyone should try it."

Holly's face lit up as she read the message on the screen. She turned toward Jean-Marc. He looked totally embarrassed.

"Oh, I'm so sorry," she blurted. "I couldn't believe it was you hassling Soozie, but I didn't know who else had access to my account. And then you were so secretive about that E-mail last night."

Jean-Marc gave a sheepish grin. "I should have let you in on what I was doing. But I guess I wasn't sure how you felt about me exactly. I was afraid if you knew how much I liked you, you might be scared off."

"Maybe we should be going," Reva suggested.

"Not yet," Nancy said. She looked apologetically at Holly and Jean-Marc. "You both seem to be in the clear. But we'll all sleep better if we can figure out how someone accessed Holly's account."

"Two cups of coffee and I still don't get it," Reva said a few hours later. She leaned back in Holly's desk chair. She rubbed her eyes with her fists. "I *know* I'm leaving out something crucial here."

"Maybe you'll do better in the morning, when you're fresher," Holly suggested. Jean-Marc had left earlier, and Holly was sitting on her bed trying to catch up on her art history reading. Soozie had stayed up talking with them, until she had finally dropped asleep on the floor.

"Holly's right, Reva. You've been at this too long," Nancy said. She had hoped Reva would have solved the puzzle by now.

"I'll never get to sleep until I figure this out," Reva said.

Nancy knew just what she meant. "I can help, but not with the technical stuff," she warned with a laugh. "But talking through a problem helps pinpoint something you've missed."

"Good idea," Reva said. "First, every single sicko note can be traced back to Holly's account."

Nancy kicked off her shoes and propped her feet up on Holly's desk. "Right. Someone came into Holly's room and used her computer. But when we checked the times the messages were sent, Holly was often here, but sometimes not."

"Nancy," Reva said, straightening up in her chair. "I never said that someone had to use Holly's computer, just her account."

"How could someone do that?" Holly wondered aloud.

"There are a couple of ways, and stealing your password is probably the most likely," Reva said excitedly. She turned to Nancy. "What did you say before about Janie?"

"She doesn't live here, so that rules her out."

"But she's still a Kappa." Reva asked Holly, "Does she know your password?"

"I don't think so," Holly answered.

"How dumb can I be?" Reva looked charged. She turned back to the keyboard and began typing. Nancy took her feet off Holly's desk, stood up, and peeked over Reva's shoulder.

"Reva, what are you thinking?" Nancy asked.

"I got sidetracked in the computer lab. I was thinking Kappas equal Kappa house. All the Kappas in the house are connected to the university's host computer directly. People just log in. But anyone off campus has to dial in to the host. That leaves a different code. And voilà!" Reva grinned. "That's it. Some of these messages sent through Holly's account came from an off-campus line. And there's only one off-campus Kappa with a Kappa E-mail address.

"It'll take a minute to find out, but . . ."

"Forget it! It's got to be Janie," Nancy said. "If we're wrong, you can go back to tracing the real culprit on the computer system." Nancy looked down at Soozie sleeping on the floor. "Don't wake up Soozie. She'll find out what's going on soon enough. But I have a feeling if we don't act on this fast, Janie's smart enough to erase her tracks. Where does she live?"

Reva read out the address.

Nancy groaned inwardly. Janie wasn't the only upperclassman who lived there. Jake did, too.

Friday night the decibel level at Jason Lehman's Club Z was at an all-time high. It was disco night and the place was in major party mode.

Eileen sat at the bar with Emmet, tapping her feet.

Jason was behind the bar with his hand over one ear, trying to have a conversation on the phone. He shook his head, then yelled something into the receiver and hung up.

"Do you know some chick named Dakota Jones, or Dallas White, or something like that?" he shouted over the music.

Eileen sagged against Emmet. "She found him," she said loudly in Emmet's ear. Turning to Jason, she said. "Not Dallas, but Montana. Montana Smith."

"She sounds like a real Froot Loop," Jason remarked, leaning over the bar.

Eileen laughed. "Good description."

"She's fun, though," Emmet told his brother.

"I don't know about that," Jason said, "but she had a great radio show tonight." The deejay switched to a slow tune, and the noise level dropped considerably. Jason went on in a more normal voice. "She called me earlier and told me I *had* to listen to it, that if I didn't my club was doomed to go from hot spot to colder than last week's leftovers. How could I ignore such a threat?"

"Jason, I tried to stop her from pestering you," Eileen said. "But Montana's got this thing for—"

"I don't know what she's got, except great taste in bands. Radical Moves is really hot. I need to get in touch with them. I want to book them, fast."

"You like Ray's band?" Emmet smiled. "Great. Ray could use a break about now."

"Ray? As in Johansson, the guy Montana interviewed tonight? You know him? Personally?"

"Sure, Jason. And Montana's tight with Ray."

"Not quite, Emmet. She only wishes she were." Eileen turned to Jason. "So, like, you're not upset or anything that she bothered you?"

"Bothered me? She did me a major favor." He frowned at Emmet. "You guys really let me down. What if Anthony's had booked them first? I would have lost out. What good are you two, anyway, if you can't get me the scoop on the hottest bands in town before some other club snatches them up?"

Jason moved off to serve another customer.

"Tell me I heard wrong. Last week we were to keep our noses out of *his* business at *his* club. This week we're supposed to be his talent scouts. Where's that dude coming from?" Emmet asked.

"Beats me," Eileen said, rolling her eyes. "Seems when it comes to Jason and this club, we can't do anything right."

"Janie, it's me, Holly." Nancy, Reva, and Holly were in the hallway on the top floor of Janie's apartment building, the building where Jake and his roommates also lived. Soft new-age music filtered out of apartment 3C. Janie was up, but Nancy wondered if she would answer at two in the morning.

Nancy heard someone check the peephole.

Then the door opened. "Holly?" Janie was still dressed. She looked past Holly's shoulder and smiled at Nancy.

Good, Nancy thought, she suspects nothing. *Or she's innocent.*

"Hi, Janie," Holly said. "Can we come in?"

"Sure." Janie acted puzzled.

"This is Reva Ross," Nancy said, introducing them as she took in Janie's studio apartment at a glance. The space was sparsely furnished with a bed by one wall, a shabby but chic-looking upholstered chair in the corner, a reading lamp, and a crate for a table. Poetry books were stacked on the table next to it. And on the desk, the computer was on.

Reva drifted over to check out the screen. "So, what brings you guys here so late?" Janie asked.

Nancy ignored the question. "Are you writing a paper?" she asked, gesturing toward the computer.

"No way." Janie laughed. "I've been surfing the chat lines. Amazing how people hook up with each other that way. Not that it's worked for me," she added with a shrug. "Seems even on the Usenet I can't buy a date." Then Janie laughed self-consciously. "Or at least with the guy I like. Bess told me to just ask him out. But by the time I worked up the nerve, he had found someone on the Usenet. Namely, our sister Soozie," Janie said bitterly.

"And the guy was TDH?" Nancy said.

Janie met Nancy's level gaze. She hesitated

only a minute. "Yeah—aka Nick O'Donnell. He's in my poetry seminar, and he won't give me the time of day."

"So you're the other TDH?" Holly asked.

Janie shrugged. "Isn't that why you're all here? How'd you figure it out?"

"You don't need to know," Reva said. "But you could look a little more upset."

"Upset?" Janie frowned. "What for? It was just a joke. And considering the way Soozie treats people, she deserved this, or worse."

"No, she didn't," Nancy said. "Crank calls, by the way, are against the law. And maybe Soozie's snobbish and self-centered and vain, but what you did on-line was beyond mean—to Soozie *and* Kappa."

Janie made a face. "For Kappa, I'm sorry. For Soozie, not really."

"But what about *this?*" Nancy said, picking up Soozie's diary. "You stole it."

"Borrowed it. I was going to return it."

"After you posted all those nasty entries on the Usenet," Holly charged. "Why did you do that?"

"I wanted the sorority to know what Soozie was really like. What she really thought about people," Janie said defiantly. "She won't be winning any popularity contests in the near future, thanks to my exposé."

Nancy couldn't believe that Janie wasn't the least bit sorry for what she had done.

"What now, Nancy?" Reva asked.

Nancy looked from Janie to Holly. "You can bring the university authorities in, or Soozie can."

"Call the authorities?" Janie balked. "No one called the authorities when Soozie threw out my clothes or humiliated me that time she found out I had a blind date and then turned up herself, said she was me, and insulted the guy in front of his friends."

"That's pretty mean stuff, Janie," Reva conceded. "I can understand where you're coming from, but threatening her on-line was way out of bounds."

Janie didn't look convinced.

Nancy asked Holly, "Doesn't the sorority have its own disciplinary board?"

"Yes," Holly said. "And Soozie—well—" Holly turned to Janie. "Maybe she did deserve to be brought down a bit, but, Janie, you really pushed the envelope here. You were wrong."

"If I'm disciplined, Soozie should be, too," Janie insisted.

Turning to Nancy, Holly said, "I'll call a hearing next week. No one got hurt, and the law wasn't really broken, was it?" she asked Reva.

Reva shrugged. "When it comes to E-mail tampering and threats over the Usenet, I'm not sure."

Nancy didn't know either. Part of her still thought Janie should be brought in front of the university authorities, at least about the phone calls. "What if Soozie goes to the university police and presses charges?" Nancy asked.

"Police?" Janie suddenly looked nervous.

"Believe me, Janie, she won't go to the police," Holly stated. "She'll just want this whole incident to go away. The less fuss she makes, the faster people will forget about those diary entries. Considering what you did, you'll probably get off much easier than you deserve."

After leaving Janie to ponder Holly's words, the girls headed downstairs. Passing the door to Jake's apartment on the floor below, Nancy stopped. "Hey, you guys, go on down. I'll catch you in a sec."

She waited until Reva and Holly were out of sight, then she lifted her hand. After a second's hesitation, she knocked on Jake's door.

Nick Dimartini, one of Jake's roommates, answered. "Nancy?" he seemed surprised to see her. He flashed her a nervous smile and pushed up his glasses. "What's up?" he asked.

"Not much," Nancy replied, peering over his shoulder. She couldn't see far into the apartment or tell if Jake was there. "Jake home?" she asked, realizing that Nick was barring the door.

"No. Not yet," Nick said evasively.

Nancy's heart stopped. It was very late on a Friday night. She could see Nick was holding something back.

"Do you know where I can catch up with him?" Nancy asked, beginning to feel very awkward.

"Uh—no. He didn't say." Nick avoided Nancy's eyes. "Want to leave a message?"

Nancy just shook her head and left. She hurried down the stairs, her mind reeling.

Was Jake on a date? Nancy pictured the waitress at Anthony's. Had Jake moved on already? Had he written her off so quickly? Had they broken up for real?

The gravel in the sweeping driveway crunched beneath the tires of the vintage MG. Stephanie pulled up to the front entrance of the Riverfront Inn. She climbed out of the leather-upholstered seat of Casey's car and handed the keys to the valet.

"I'll be staying for dinner," she told him. Or at least I *hope* I will, she added to herself. She tipped him generously. Whenever she felt nervous, she was lavish with money. He got in the car, but she could feel his eyes on her as she strode up the short flight of steps and through the double doors of Weston's most exclusive restaurant.

Stephanie knew she looked terrific in a short, clingy black dress that showed her figure to advantage and set off her stunning dark hair. Inside, though, she felt like a perfect mess. Casey's plan had sounded great, but would it work?

In the lounge just off the main dining room, she spotted Jonathan. He was dressed in a business suit, his briefcase beside him, on the sofa. If Stephanie's whole future weren't at stake, she might have burst out laughing. He looked so nervous. But who could blame him?

Disguising her voice, Casey had called him earlier that day, saying she was from the employment office of the largest retail store in the Weston Mall. She wanted to interview him for a possible position as store manager. The job would be open in a couple of weeks, and she was determined to fill it quickly. She had heard great things about Jonathan Baur from Berrigan's and needed to talk to him immediately before she checked out some other prospects. She had set up the interview over dinner at the inn.

Tossing her hair back from her face and checking herself in a mirror, Stephanie bypassed the maitre d' and walked right up to Jonathan.

"Stephanie?" He looked baffled for a second. "What are you doing here?" he asked, his voice tightening. "I have a business appointment." He checked his watch and frowned.

"I know." Stephanie sat down and crossed her shapely legs.

"What do you mean, you know?"

"Because," she said, taking a deep breath, "I'm the appointment. The Weston Mall isn't interested in you," she said sweetly. "But I am."

Jonathan took a second to digest what was happening. "Is this some kind of joke?" he finally said, getting up slowly.

Stephanie jumped up with him. "No, Jonathan. I'm not joking at all. But I couldn't figure out another way to get a chance to talk to you."

The anger on Jonathan's face shifted quickly to suspicion to disbelief to resignation. "I've been had," he said, not very warmly. "So you want to talk, do you?"

The fact that he didn't just turn his back and walk away gave Stephanie the courage to go on. "Yes. But not just talk. We've tried that," Stephanie said earnestly. "I wanted to try something new. I thought, maybe, we could start all over again and make this Stephanie and Jonathan, take two. What do you say we pretend that this is our first date?"

Jonathan looked skeptical. "Too much has happened, Stephanie. I can't pretend you never cheated. The first time you promised to stop, I believed you. Why should I believe you now?"

"Because I'm asking you to," Stephanie said simply. Hesitantly, she reached for his hand and took it between both of hers. She felt his resistance begin to break down. "Oh, Jonathan, all I want is a chance to turn over a new leaf. I know I've acted terribly, but it's only because I've been afraid."

Jonathan searched her eyes. "I know that. I won't leave you, Stephanie, if you don't force me to."

"I won't. Because there's only one thing I want, Jonathan, and that's love. And thick-headed, crazy, spoiled brat that I am, I didn't realize until now I've really found it with you." When she looked up at Jonathan, he was wearing the most wonderful smile. Just as he bent his head to kiss her, the maitre d' came up and offered to show them to their table. Stephanie held out her hand to Jonathan. He hesitated only a moment, then began to laugh. "I feel helpless. Tricked. And totally happy."

The maitre d' led the way toward the candlelit dining room, but Jonathan held Stephanie back. "But, Steph," he said in a panicky voice, "I can't afford this place."

"Me either," she admitted with a giggle. "But it's all taken care of—I'll explain later. Meanwhile, let's just enjoy our first date. Remember," she told him coyly, "we don't know each other at all yet."

"Of course not," Jonathan said, slipping easily into the game. "In fact, I've been dying to ask you out. But," he said, "I couldn't get reservations here until now."

"So," she asked, after they had ordered, "tell me about yourself."

"Haven't we tried this once before?" Jonathan asked. "You were supposed to tell me one big secret about yourself and you didn't."

Stephanie pretended to look surprised. "I've never met you before, I've just dreamed of someone like you all my life. But if you want to know a secret . . ." Stephanie thought back to the night a month or so before when she and Jonathan were at the lake. He had told her some harmless story about when he was a kid. But she had felt too vulnerable to reveal to him even the silliest thing about herself. Stephanie was determined to make tonight different. "For one year—and one year only—I was a Girl Scout. I even earned a merit badge."

"You?" The expression on Jonathan's face was worth making a fool of herself. "I don't believe it."

"Would I lie—on a first date?"

"I don't know you well enough yet to say," Jonathan replied.

"You will," Stephanie said, running a finger down the back of his hand. "Where was I? Oh yes, Girl Scout camp. I hated it, by the way."

"I bet. What was the merit badge for? Makeup?" Jonathan teased.

"Not even close,'" Stephanie said, leaning provocatively over the table. "For wilderness survival. My troop had to stay overnight in the middle of the woods and find its way back to camp. Some idiot lost the map. Everyone panicked. But not me," Stephanie announced with relish. "I single-handedly got us back in record time."

"How'd you do it?" Jonathan asked, impressed.

"I was very highly motivated. Imagine me living without a shower and clean hair for more than twenty-four hours," she announced, cracking Jonathan up.

He reached across the table for her hand. "What other surprises do you have in store for me?"

The warmth in his eyes made Stephanie's soul

sing. "If I told," she said, demurring, "they wouldn't be surprises."

As they were leaving, Stephanie told him about Casey, how she'd paid for the whole evening in advance because she was sick of seeing Stephanie moping over Jonathan. "Tricking you here with the promise of a job interview was her idea, you know."

"That was *her* on the phone?" Jonathan whistled under his breath. "I didn't recognize her voice."

"She got the idea from an episode of *The President's Daughter*. The plot had to do with two star-crossed lovers who weren't on speaking terms."

"Star-crossed lovers?" Jonathan shook his head. "Not us, Stephanie. Not anymore," he said, outside the entrance to the inn.

"And never again," Stephanie promised as they sealed their promise with a kiss.

CHAPTER 14

"Today, first thing, I'm changing my password," Holly told Jean-Marc late Saturday morning. He'd dropped by to pick her up for brunch. Holly was at her desk keying some information into her computer.

"Why are you changing it?" Jean-Marc asked, pulling up a chair.

"Because that's how Janie broke into my account, making it look like *I* was tormenting Soozie. She told me this morning when I called to set up her disciplinary hearing."

"Janie Covington was TDH?" Jean-Marc whistled. Jean-Marc had left Kappa the previous night, before Reva and Nancy had singled out Janie as the culprit. "I didn't think she knew enough about computers to pull that off. How did she figure out your password anyway?"

"First, about the password." Holly scrunched up her face. "That was my fault. I broke the number-one rule in choosing one." She tapped the photo of her cat over her desk. "I used *Petals*."

Understanding dawned on Jean-Marc's face. "So if Janie ever came in here, she saw the name under the picture of your cat."

"And Janie's been in my room plenty over the past couple of years. Meanwhile, I've learned lesson one. Never use the name of a pet for a password." Holly tapped a few more keys, then turned off her computer. "That's done. Now no one, not even you, will ever know what it is."

Holly proceeded to tell Jean-Marc about how they'd traced everything back to Janie. "She admitted to it right away."

"But why did she do it?"

"Because she was really furious with Soozie. Then when Soozie tried to scare you and me out of meeting each other in person, after we hooked up on-line, Janie decided to give her a dose of her own medicine."

"And like everyone else around here, she knew Soozie's handle," Jean-Marc recalled. "And Nick O'Donnell's, too."

"At first when she tapped into Soozie's E-mail, Janie just intended to make her nervous, but then when she realized the poems TDH was sending Soozie were from whatever she'd been studying in her poetry class, she realized TDH was Nick. She had a major crush on Nick herself."

Jean-Marc chuckled. "She must have hit the roof."

"Really." Holly joined in, laughing. "But then

Janie went too far," she added, growing serious. "She began plaguing the house with midnight phone calls, not thinking that everyone else would get freaked, too. She was just trying to scare Soozie so bad that she'd never have the nerve to meet Nick in person."

"Well, I can't say I feel too sorry for Soozie, and I hope Janie doesn't get in too much trouble over this," Jean-Marc told Holly. "Though I'm really upset she tried to lay blame on you."

"Me, too," Holly said softly. "I've always stuck up for her around the house. What if Reva had never been able to trace the E-mail back to Janie? I would have looked guilty."

"I still don't understand how she made the E-mail look as though you'd sent it."

Holly explained about overriding address commands. "I don't know how it works, really. And actually, Reva was surprised that Janie knew how to do it. But it turns out that Janie has taken a slew of computer courses."

"So what happens to her now?"

"I don't know, Jean-Marc. Kicking her out of Kappa won't do much. She doesn't even live here anymore. And actually everyone on the disciplinary committee is sort of glad Soozie got her just deserts. We've decided to double Janie's community service, and maybe we'll come up with something more."

As Holly got up to get her coat, Jean-Marc put his hands on her shoulders. "Aren't you really upset about Janie, using you like that?"

Holly nodded. "Yes."

"I'm not sure about this sorority business. You women are not always nice to each other in this house. Soozie sometimes treats people like dirt, and Janie was pretty disloyal."

Holly thought a moment. "I can't defend either of them, really. But there are other things about being in a sorority. In the long run we really are there for each other. And Kappa does have a code of honor that I respect and try to live by. Most of the girls do, most of the time."

"Well, if you're happy with Kappa, then I'm happy you are a Kappa. I must say, though, I'm glad you didn't let Stylish Sister Soozie talk you out of meeting *me.*"

"Me, too," Holly said from the bottom of her heart. She gazed into his blue eyes. "Me, too," she repeated. And just to show him how glad she was, she drew his face down toward hers and gave him a long, sweet kiss.

Soozie stood on one side of the soda machine outside the Graves Hall computer lab. Nick stood on the other. Soozie had never felt so awkward and embarrassed. Everyone knew about her diary now. She felt exposed.

"I'm surprised you agreed to talk to me out here," Soozie said, unable to meet Nick's eyes. She wasn't sure if he had seen the postings on the Usenet about her Kappa sisters.

Nick shifted from foot to foot. "Well, I'm surprised that someone would go to all that trouble to make it look like I was some kind of chat-room creep."

Soozie heard the anger in his voice. "Actually, it's all over and done with. It was just a dirty trick." She put her hand tentatively on Nick's arm and forced herself to look at his face. "I'm sorry a nice guy like you got involved in it."

"Nice guy?" Nick's eyebrows arched up. "Now, that's an improvement. You used to think I was just a geek."

Soozie grimaced. "But, Nick, I told you the other night, I don't now. I haven't since I read your first few messages—I mean TDH's *real* ones," she said. She would never forgive Janie for this one. And she wondered if her other Kappa sisters would forgive her for her diary.

Soozie decided then and there she'd better do something about her situation in Kappa house. One did catch more flies with honey than vinegar. She truly hadn't intended for anyone to see that diary. Somehow she had to find a way to win back the respect—if not the friendship—of her sisters.

But at the moment she didn't care as much about Kappa as about this really nice guy stand-ing next to her—a guy she hoped to date. But now, would he even want to bother with her?

"So then, where do we go from here?" Nick suddenly asked.

"I don't know," Soozie began seriously. "I'd like to pick up where we left off the other night. I'd like to get to know you better face-to-face."

"Ah. You want to know the real TDH?"

Soozie gave an involuntary shudder. "No. I don't," she said, then arched one eyebrow. "But I wouldn't mind getting to know the real Nick O'Donnell this morning over brunch."

"Sounds perfect to me, Sweet Sister Soozie—"

"That's not what my handle stands for," Soozie said, starting to correct him, then stopping. *Sweet* suddenly felt better than *Stylish.* "But I think I like it better," she told him as they strolled arm in arm to Java Joe's.

"You were sure right about one thing, George," Nancy said. "A good run does help put things in perspective." It was late Saturday morning, and Nancy and George were at Thayer after a long jog around the campus. During their workout, she'd poured her heart out about Jake. George's commonsense take on things had grounded Nancy.

"I'm sure you were jumping to conclusions about that waitress. I told you Bess and I ran into Jake the other day. He kept asking about you. I think he was trying to find out if we knew how you were feeling about him."

"Right," Nancy said.

"And that's when Bess sort of blew up at him. She's not doing well lately," George confided.

"I'll call and check up on her later," Nancy said. "Maybe we can rent a video and hang out together this afternoon."

Nancy ducked into her closet for a change of clothes.

"Hey, Nan, your answering machine is flashing," George called out to her.

Nancy zipped up her jeans, and pulled on a white V-neck T-shirt. She punched a button on her machine.

"Nancy?" Terry Schneider's deep voice brought a smile to her lips. "It's me, Terry. Sorry I haven't been around. The film festival's been taking all my time. Everything okay? Anyway, don't forget FFS is screening the next Fellini movie tonight. Want to join me? I'd better warn you, though. I'm leading the discussion again. Call me . . . or I'll try you later."

Before Nancy could think about Terry's offer, the next message began. "Nancy, it's me." Jake sounded cautious. "I heard you dropped by last night. Sorry I missed you. Give me a call." The machine clicked off.

Nancy stared in dismay at the phone. Was that all he had to say?

"What are you going to do?" George's voice jolted Nancy back to the present.

"I don't know." Nancy said. "I have so much to work out with Jake. I should call him and meet him somewhere. But I also want to go to that Fellini movie. I really loved the last one."

"So go," George urged.

"Jake would hit the roof—again. Remember the last scene he made when he saw me with

Terry? Jake will take it as a big rejection. He's so jealous."

"But, Nancy, going to the film with Terry wouldn't be a date, would it?"

"Of course not," Nancy insisted. "We're just friends. But I've been thinking of giving up my friendship with Terry. That just might ease the way for Jake and me to work out our differences."

"Why should you drop Terry? I mean, *he's* not the problem. If you and Jake were on solid ground, Terry's friendship with you wouldn't bother Jake one bit."

"I know," Nancy conceded sadly. "But now what do I do?" She looked at George. "Go to the movies with Terry, which is what I'd love to do? Or try to be with Jake?"

"I can't tell you what to do, Nancy," George said with a twinkle in her eye. "I'll only tell you not to make such a big deal of it."

Nancy managed a smile. Not such a big deal? If only George were right. Nancy turned her back on George and picked up the phone. Maybe there was no choice to be made here. Slowly, she dialed a number.

Nancy's heart raced as the phone began to ring.

"Hello?"

At the sound of the deep, familiar male voice on the other end, Nancy began to smile.

"Hi," she said. "It's me, Nancy."

Next in Nancy Drew on Campus™:

The heat's on between Nancy and Jake. Romance? No way. Anger? Jealousy? Resentment? You bet! And just because Nancy went to the movies with Terry. Maybe it's time to cool it with Jake, like George is doing with Will. He thinks she's found another guy, too. But the truth is far more complicated . . . and far more scary! Meanwhile, Ginny Yuen, who's volunteering at the hospital, can't figure out what's going on with the handsome young doctor Malcolm Hendrix. Is it chemistry or is it a con? The truth may come out in an exposé Nancy's writing for the *Wilder Times*. But Nancy has to deal with Jake's jealousy and her own: her old boyfriend, Ned, is coming to Wilder—to see Bess . . . in *Jealous Feelings*, Nancy Drew on Campus #20.